Andrew Klavan has been hailed by ~~Stephen~~ King as 'the most original novelist of crime and suspense since Cornell Woolrich'. He is the winner of two Edgar Awards and the author of such bestsellers as *True Crime* (adapted for film by Clint Eastwood), *Don't Say A Word* (adapted as a film starring Michael Douglas), and *Empire of Lies*.

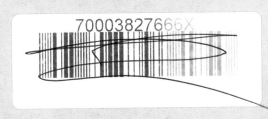

The HOMELANDER series by Andrew Klavan

THE FINAL HOUR

ANDREW KLAVAN

headline

First published in Great Britain in 2011 by
HEADLINE PUBLISHING GROUP

1

Cataloguing in Publication Data is available from the British Library

ISBN 978 0 7553 5302 6

Typeset in Aldine401BT by Avon DataSet Ltd,
Bidford-on-Avon, Warwickshire

Printed in the UK by CPI Mackays, Chatham, ME5 8TD

Headline's policy is to use papers that are natural, renewable and
recyclable products and made from wood grown in sustainable forests.
The logging and manufacturing processes are expected to conform to the
environmental regulations of the country of origin.

HEADLINE PUBLISHING GROUP
An Hachette UK Company
338 Euston Road
London NW1 3BH

www.headline.co.uk
www.hachette.co.uk

This book is for Conor Hudnut

THE FINAL HOUR

PART I

Chapter One

Abingdon

Most people have to die to get to hell. I took a short cut.

I was in Abingdon State Prison. Locked away for a murder I didn't commit. Waiting for the men who were coming to kill me. With nowhere to run.

It was the worst thing that had ever happened to me.

I'd been there for two weeks. Two weeks of smothering boredom and strangling fear. When I was locked in my cell, the minutes seemed to lie like dead men, to decay like dead men – so slowly you could barely tell it was happening. When I was out in the exercise yard or in the cafeteria or in the showers, there was just the fear, the waiting. Waiting for the killers to make good their threat, remembering the words one of them had whispered in my ear as I stood in the dinner line one night: *You're already dead, West. You just don't know it yet.*

Alone in my cell, I stared at the tan wall. I felt a black despair surrounding me, closing in on me. I did everything I could to fight it. I did push-ups. I read my Bible. I prayed.

The prayer gave me some comfort, some relief.

But then the buzzer would sound, loud and startling. The cell door would slide open. A guard would shout from the end of the tier, 'Yard time!'

Then the waiting and the fear would begin again.

Where was Detective Rose? I wondered desperately. I hadn't seen him since he'd arrested me, since he'd rescued me from the Homelanders' terrorist cell and led me away in handcuffs. Rose was the one official who knew who I was. He knew I'd been planted in the Homelanders by Waterman and his agents. He knew I'd let myself be framed for the murder of my friend, Alex Hauser, so the Homelanders would believe I was bitter and could be recruited. Rose was one of Waterman's agents too – at least, I thought he was. I told myself he must be working behind the scenes to clear my name, to win my release. I told myself he would come for me. Any day now. Any day.

But the killers came for me first.

I was in the exercise yard. It was a large square of dying grass and broken asphalt. It was surrounded by a fence topped with barbed wire. The fence was surrounded by a high concrete wall. At the corners of the wall there were guard towers. In the towers there were men with rifles, watching our every move.

Here, below, on the grass and asphalt, the prisoners moved in their gray uniforms. Some wore shirtsleeves, but most wore gray overcoats and black woolen watchcaps against the snow-flecked cold. Each coat or shirt had a white strip with the prisoner's number on it, sewn over the left breast. Each had the prisoner's name stenciled over the right breast. Other than that, they were all gray.

The men's faces, on the other hand, were black and white and brown. Their eyes were hard and watchful. There was rage and meanness and fear etched into the tight lines of their cheeks and foreheads. They gathered around the benches and free weights on one corner of the asphalt or played basketball on the half-court, or played catch on the grass or just walked and talked or just sat and stared.

Guards moved among them: men in blue shirts and black pants. They carried no weapons, just heavy walkie-talkies hooked to their belts. The guards watched the prisoners but the prisoners didn't watch the guards. The prisoners watched each other. And some of them, I knew, were watching me, waiting for their chance to attack.

I was on one of the weight benches. I was doing presses with a light bar, not trying to bulk up or anything, just trying to keep the flexibility and speed I used in my karate training. The men all around me were going for the big muscle stuff, lifting hundreds of pounds. They worked in grim silence. Whenever I dared to steal a glance at one of them, they looked like pretty nasty pieces of work. White guys with shaved heads and thick arms and chests. They had Nazi swastikas tattooed on their biceps and on their foreheads. A couple of them had Christian crosses tattooed on them too. How they thought those two symbols could ever go together – a symbol of hatred and a symbol of love – I didn't know. I'll tell you

5

what else: I wasn't about to ask. They didn't look like the type of guys who would enjoy a good theological conversation. They looked more like the type of guys who would enjoy punching me repeatedly in the face until I lost consciousness or died. That sounded like it would be more fun for them than for me, so I kept my mouth shut.

When I finished my workout, I moved away from them. I wandered to the edge of the crumbling basketball court, glancing this way and that to make sure no one was coming after me. I stood by the court and watched the game, feeling the cold air dry the workout sweat on my cheeks and neck.

The game was three against three. They were good players: rough, fast, with accurate shots from anywhere near the key. They swirled back and forth in front of me in a shouting gray cloud of motion. They elbowed each other in the face, and jostled each other shoulder to chest as they fought for position under the board.

One guy broke through and went airborne, jamming a dunk through the hoop. As the teams reset, I took another nervous glance over my shoulder at the yard behind me. But, this time, something made me pause.

The guards. Suddenly I didn't see any guards. The blue shirts that usually passed among the gray uniforms had vanished. I felt an instinctive clutch inside me, a flash of something like panic. Where had they all gone?

The next moment, the killers struck.

There were three of them. They were black men. In prison,

the Muslims were mostly black. They weren't your regular, everyday Muslims either. They were hate-filled radical Islamists.

The Islamists had heard about me on the grapevine and in the news. The word was I'd betrayed the Homelanders, a group of Islamo-fascists who recruited disgruntled Americans to pull off terrorist attacks on our home soil. The Abingdon prison Islamists had vowed they'd take vengeance on me. They'd see to it that I was punished for trying to protect my country. This was their time.

The first one came at me with a shiv – a knife he'd made by sharpening a piece of hard plastic he'd smuggled out of the cafeteria. He strode up to me from the right and drove the point in low toward my side.

I caught the motion out of the corner of my eye. I swung around fast, blocking with my forearm, blocking instinctively with the reflexes I'd developed during all those years of training at the dojo. Those reflexes saved my life – for the moment, anyway.

My forearm hit the killer's arm. The plastic shiv sliced in front of me, missing my mid-section by inches. Off balance, I managed a weak kick at the attacker's leg. It hit him high, above the knee, and only knocked him back a step or two.

Then the others grabbed me from behind.

There were two of them: big, strong. I never got a good look at them. I just felt their breath on the sides of my face. They each grabbed one of my arms, wrapping their own arms around it, holding it fast. They pressed their bodies hard against me, blocking off my legs with their legs so I couldn't kick again. I couldn't move at all. I was helpless.

The man with the shiv came back for me.

I got a good look at him now. He was enormous: tall and broad-shouldered, with huge muscles that pressed through the prison grays. He had a long, thin face that reminded me of a wolf's face. His eyes were bright with wolf-like hunger and bloodlust.

He grinned as his friends caught hold of me.

'Hold him,' he told them. Then he said to me, 'Now you die, traitor.'

I tried to pull my arms free, tried to kick out with my legs. It was useless. The men who held me were too strong.

The man with the shiv stepped toward me, the sharpened point aimed at my stomach.

I had only one more second – just enough time to realize I was about to die – just enough time for that information to flash red-hot through my brain.

Then the man's wolf-like face filled my vision, blotted out everything else. There was nothing but his grin and his eyes.

But, all at once, his eyes flew up, went white, empty. His grin vanished and his mouth dropped open, slack. He staggered back away from me. I saw his legs go wobbly. I saw his knees buckle.

He collapsed on to the grass with a hollow thud. The plastic shiv fell from his limp fingers.

Chapter Two

The Yard King

What just happened?

In the terror of the moment, I couldn't make sense of it. Then I could.

One of the Nazi musclemen – one of the thugs who'd been with me by the free weights – was standing before me where the wolf-faced man had been. His fist was raised; a stone was gripped in it. He had stepped up behind the Islamist assassin and clubbed him in the back of the neck.

The next instant, the two men holding me were ripped away, as if they'd been caught up in a tornado or something. Some swastika-tattooed musclemen had grabbed them, dragging them off me. As the men fought back, more of the Islamists were running to the scene to join the fight, and more of the Nazis too. Another second and hate-filled men were battling other hate-filled men back and forth across the grass. There was the crack of fists on bone; blood flying through the air; grunted curses and ugly names. Men down on the ground rolling over and over one another, trying

9

to gouge one another's eyes or clutch one another's throats.

It all happened in a second. I stood dazed at the center of the chaos.

I thought, *This is hell. It must look just like this in hell.*

Now the guards in their blue shirts seemed suddenly to reappear out of nowhere. They rushed into the melee of gray uniforms, wrapping arms around prisoners' throats to pull them apart, hammering at their heads with the edges of their walkie-talkies, kicking at them as they rolled around in the dirt and on the asphalt.

Shouting and striking out, the guards drove the Nazis and Islamists away from each other, forcing them into opposite areas of the yard.

It was all over as quickly as it began. I hardly had time to register what had happened, to compute the fact that this prison feud had saved my life. One hate group had fought off another hate group and somehow the result was that I was still standing, still alive.

Still alive – but my troubles were far from over.

Because, now, across the grass, the Yard King was coming.

That's what they called him: the Yard King. His real name was Chuck Dunbar. He was Corrections Officer in charge of the Prisoner Recreation Area, the chief guard of the exercise yard. He wasn't a big man but he packed a lot of nastiness into his thick, five-foot-seven frame. He was squat and broad and had a face like the business end of a fist, all mean and knuckly. His headquarters was a place known as *The Outbuilding*. It was a grim, featureless cinder-block box that stood in the furthest corner of the yard. Dunbar spent most of his time in there, doing whatever it was he did. But when there was trouble – or when he wanted to start trouble – out he came. The sight of him was always bad news for someone, because the Yard King was a man who liked hurting people.

And right now, he was coming straight at me.

He barreled forward fast with his peculiar rolling walk, his lips twisted in a snarl, his fists clenched by his sides. His eyes were pale, almost colorless, but they seemed to burn as if they were lit with white flames.

Another second or two and he was standing in front of me. The rest of the guards lined up on either side of him. The Yard King glanced to his left and to his right.

'Get this con garbage back in their cells,' he growled.

Instantly, the guards started moving, started screaming at the prisoners, striking out at them and herding them toward the prison doors. The men moved sullenly, their gray shoulders hunched. They cast wicked glances at each other, muttering threats through the gaps between the guards.

I started moving too, figuring I was supposed to go back to my cell as well.

But Dunbar stepped in close to me, blocking my way.

'Not you, lowlife,' he said. He had a voice like a rake on gravel. It seemed to rattle inside his throat as it came out at me. 'You're the one who started this.'

'Me?' I blurted out. 'I was just standing here. That guy tried to kill me. He had a knife. He—'

The Yard King hit me in the face. He used the back of his

11

hand, snapping it fast at my cheek. My head flew back, my thoughts rattled.

'Shut up,' Dunbar said. 'Don't lie to me.'

I rubbed my bruised cheek. It didn't seem like a good idea to answer him, so I didn't.

Dunbar smiled, his eyes flashing. 'How could anyone have a knife in the yard?' he asked me. 'If someone had a knife in the yard, that would mean they'd gotten it past one of my guards. That would mean there was something wrong with the way I run this place. You think there's something wrong with the way I run this place, punk?'

I went on rubbing my cheek. I went on not answering. But that wasn't good enough for the Yard King.

This time, when he struck out at me, my hand was in his way, and blocked the blow. But I still felt the jar of it.

'I asked you a question, lowlife,' Dunbar said. 'You think I'm not doing my job right? You want to file a complaint with the authorities?'

I tried to think of something to say. But all I could think of was the way things used to be, the life I used to have. I flashed back on how things were when I was at home. I thought of the way my parents and pastors and teachers and my karate instructor, Sensei Mike, would always tell me to tell the truth, no matter what. It seemed like only yesterday I was back in that world, and yet it seemed like a million years ago. Back there, back home, there weren't any guys like Chuck Dunbar – or, if there were, I didn't know them and they didn't have complete and total control over my life. Back home, it was easy to say, 'Tell the truth no matter what,' when 'no matter what' didn't include a guy who would gladly break every bone in your body and never pay a price.

Still, I didn't say anything. I couldn't think of anything to say.

Dunbar smiled again, a weird, dreamy smile full of cruelty and a sick pleasure in cruelty. 'Charlie West,' he said. My name sounded pretty bad when he spoke it, like the name of some kind of slimy creature you wouldn't want to find crawling on you. 'You think you're pretty special, don't you, Charlie West? I watch you. I know you. You think you're something better than the rest of us.'

'I don't—'

He hit me again, not hard, just enough to make me shut up – and shut up is exactly what I did.

'You're nothing,' Dunbar said, his pale eyes gleaming. 'You're not even nothing. You're a piece of garbage blowing across the yard. I'm going to teach you that, West. I'm going to make it my special mission to teach you. I'm going to make it my hobby, my pastime. From now on, the slightest thing you do, the first wrong move, the first wrong word that comes out of your mouth, I'm taking you into the Outbuilding.'

I stood up straight when I heard that, my heart clutching with fear. The Outbuilding. Every prisoner in Abingdon knew what that meant. The Outbuilding was where the Yard King took you when he wanted to teach you a lesson, when he wanted to work you over, hard, with his fists or with a club. Tucked away in the shadow of the yard wall, the building

13

was only partially visible from one of the guard towers. Once you were inside, no one could see what was happening to you and no one would ever tell. It was the heart of the Yard King's sadistic kingdom.

'Now, I asked you a question, garbage,' he said. 'How could a con in this yard have a knife when I'm in charge of keeping the place safe? You think I'm not doing my job, garbage? You think I made a mistake? Answer me.'

I know: I should have answered him. I should have just lied and said no. I should have said, 'No, sir. You're doing a great job.' I should have said, 'There was no knife, sir. There couldn't have been a knife, sir. Because you don't make mistakes, sir.'

That's what I should have said. But somehow . . . as far away from home as I was . . . somehow I just couldn't forget what my mom and dad and Sensei Mike had taught me. I couldn't force the lie up out of my throat. It stuck there, sour and disgusting. All I could do was stand and stare into the fist-like face of this cruel, sick little man.

Dunbar grinned. 'What are you waiting for, garbage? You think someone's gonna help you? No one's gonna help you. Not in here. In here, you're all alone.'

I didn't mean to talk back to him, so help me. I meant to be smart and stay quiet. But before I could stop myself, the words just sort of came out.

'I'm not alone,' I told him. 'I'm never alone.'

Dunbar's face twisted in rage. This time, when he lifted his hand, he was holding a stun gun. I saw it only for an instant, then a teeth-jarring blast of agony went through me. My brain turned to cotton. My muscles turned to rubber.

I felt myself falling and falling.

Chapter Three

Into the Past

I don't know how long it was before the guards hurled me on to the floor of my cell. It might have been a long time. It might have just felt like a long time.

When the cell door clanged shut behind me, I lay where I was, bruised and battered and bleeding.

Dunbar had taken me into the Outbuilding. He had beat me, hard: punched me, kicked me, slammed my face into the cement floor. He enjoyed it. You could tell by the gleam in his colorless eyes.

When he was finished with me, he called out the door to his guards. A couple of them came in and grabbed me under the arms. They dragged me out of the Outbuilding, my head hanging down, my toes scraping against the concrete floor. They dragged me into the prison, cursing my dead weight the whole way.

They dragged me up a flight of rattling metal stairs, then down the second-tier gallery. The prisoners watched me from inside their cells, watched dead-eyed and silent as I was dragged past.

When we reached my cell, the barred door slid open. The guards tossed me inside, the way you'd toss an old mattress on to a junk heap. I grunted as I landed on the floor. I heard the door slide shut behind me. I lay there and bled.

Images drifted through my mind. Memories. Faces. My mom and dad. My sister. My friends Josh, the goofy nerd, and big Rick, the gentle giant, and Miler Miles, the runner who would be a CEO someday.

And Beth. Beth, with her honey hair and her blue eyes and her soft lips that I could almost feel on mine. Beth and me walking together on the path by the river. Not me as I was now, beaten and frightened and wallowing in hopelessness, but the guy I used to be, walking with her, hand in hand . . .

I remembered the night before my blackout: the night I remembered going to sleep in my own bed. I was excited because, earlier that day, I had worked up the courage to talk to Beth for the first time and she'd written her phone number on my arm. I remembered how I looked around my room once before I turned the lights off, my eyes passing over the karate trophies on the shelves and the poster from the movie *Lord of the Rings* on the wall. I remembered closing my eyes with the soft bed under me and the warm blankets around me. Home. Safe at home.

When I opened my eyes again, everything I knew and loved had disappeared. The Homelanders were trying to kill me. The police wanted to arrest me for murder. A year of my life seemed to have vanished into thin air. It wasn't until later that I found out I had taken a drug to wipe out my memory so that the Homelanders couldn't get the secrets of Waterman's team out of me.

Before he died – before the Homelanders killed him – Waterman had given me an antidote to the amnesia drug: another drug to make those memories return. They returned, all right, in sudden attacks that were sometimes accompanied by spasms of terrible, gripping pain. Those 'memory attacks' still overwhelmed me sometimes and I dreaded them. But, bit by bit, they were giving me back the life I had lost: the truth about myself. I was grateful for that.

The memories I was having now though – now as I lay on the cell floor – these were different. I felt no pain as I saw the faces of the people I loved – or, that is, the only pain I felt was the pain of being unable to reach out and touch them, to hear their voices, to be with them. Because I had been processed back into prison as a fugitive, I had hardly gotten to see anyone before I was locked away. I was in court just long enough to see Beth and my mother crying in the benches, to see my father just barely holding himself together, my friends raising fists of encouragement while their eyes registered despair.

Then I was brought here to Abingdon. I was allowed to call my lawyer, but that was it: you had to earn other phone privileges through good behavior. I hadn't even gotten a visiting day yet so I hadn't seen any of the people I loved. I felt as if they might as well be on the far side of the moon.

Remembering, I continued to lie where I was. The blood

ran out of my nose and out of a cut on my forehead. It pooled, damp and thick and sticky, around my face. I wanted to get up. I wanted to clean myself off. But I couldn't muster the strength to move. I just lay there and let the images pass.

Finally, after a while, I managed to pray a little, in a confused sort of dreamy way. I didn't ask God to send angels down from the sky to lift me out of here or anything like that. I knew the world didn't work that way. I knew God made people free and gave them choices and I knew that meant they could do bad stuff to each other if they wanted to. Maybe life would be easier if we were all just God-zombies doing what was right automatically. But no one ever said freedom was easy.

So I just prayed God would keep his hand in my hand. I knew he knew what it was like to have people do unfair things to you and to hurt you for their own reasons. I just prayed he would stand next to my mom and dad and next to Beth and my friends and whisper to them that he remembered what it felt like, that he knew.

Things come into your head when you pray, I've noticed. Helpful things, almost like messages. Right now, for instance, I remembered the Churchill card – the index card Sensei Mike had given me. He'd written some words on the card, words once spoken by the British Prime Minister, Winston Churchill: a speech he'd given during World War II when it seemed the Nazis might destroy his country forever.

'Never give in; never give in – never, never, never, never, in nothing great or small, large or petty, never give in except to convictions of honor and good sense. Never yield to force: never yield to the apparently overwhelming might of the enemy.'

Somehow the words made me feel a little better. They made me feel good about not giving Dunbar the lie he wanted to hear. He had the 'overwhelming might of the enemy,' that was for sure. He could beat me up as much as he wanted and there wasn't anything I could do to stop him. But the truth – the truth belonged to me. It was mine, and I hadn't let him take it from me.

Lying on the floor in my own blood, I closed my hand. It was funny: I would almost swear I felt another hand in mine.

I'm not alone, Dunbar, I thought. *I'm never alone.*

I found the strength to rise.

Groaning, I got to my knees. I took hold of the edge of my cot. I pulled myself up and climbed slowly to my feet. I hobbled slowly to the steel sink in the corner and washed my face, watching the blood swirl down the drain. When I raised my eyes to the small square of mirror on the wall, the sight wasn't pretty. I was purple and swollen and cut, but at least the bleeding had stopped.

I went back to my cot and dropped down on to the thin mattress. I stretched out on my back and lay staring up at the white concrete ceiling. The faces of the people I loved and missed rose up before me again and then . . .

Then, with a sort of flash, there was something else.

A dark night. A torrential rain. A flash of lightning.

I blinked, shaking my head. This was more like a vision than a memory. For one flashing second, that rainy night had seemed real, it had seemed to surround me.

I breathed deeply, slowly, hoping that would be all there was. I didn't I think I was strong enough to go through a memory attack right now. But then . . .

Then there it was again. Another flash. The dark night on every side of me. The rain lanced down at the windows. They were the grated windows of a bus. A prison bus. It was rumbling and shuddering around me.

I understood what this was. Of course. I had been in prison once before. I had been convicted of murdering my friend, Alex Hauser. I'd been convicted of plunging a knife into his chest after we had an argument over Beth. It was a frame-up, a false accusation: all part of Waterman's plan to get me into the Homelanders, to convince them that I was ready to join their terrorist crew. After my arrest . . .

I remembered now. I had been in a local jail for about a week. Then they'd put me on a bus to transfer me somewhere else. Here. They were going to send me here, to Abingdon.

Reality seemed to flicker on and off. The past – that rainy night, the shuddering bus – seemed to flicker in and out of being around me.

'Yes,' I whispered to myself. 'Yes, I remember now . . .'

I started to sit up on the cot.

But then I doubled over in pain as the full memory attack struck me.

Chapter Four

Broadside

It was so real. It wasn't like a memory at all. It was just as if I were there, on the bus, in the night, in the storm.

I was the only passenger on the long gray-green vehicle. The only other people here were the guard and the driver. The guard sat in a cage up front, cradling a shotgun on his lap. The driver was almost out of sight, just the top of his head showing over the big seat before the wheel.

We were on a small road, a rough road. The bus rocked and bounced as it went over potholes. I was jostled back and forth, my shoulder hitting the window. For some reason, I couldn't brace myself properly. I looked down to find out why. I was wearing an orange prison jumper – and I was in shackles, my hands cuffed, my feet chained. My body was flung from side to side, striking the window grate just as lightning forked through the black sky, illuminating the slashing downpour for one trembling second.

I noticed something else now too: my heart was beating hard. I was nervous, excited, afraid. Something was about to happen. I didn't know exactly what it was and I didn't know exactly when it would begin, but I sensed it would be soon.

It came to me: Rose had told me the Homelanders were already working to break me out. He said they'd probably act fast before I was too closely guarded, surrounded with security.

This seemed like a good time, out on this bleak, empty road, alone on this bus with only one guard and one driver.

But, even though I was expecting it at any moment, it was a shock when it actually happened.

Suddenly, the windows exploded with blinding light. I turned and saw headlights glaring at me like a beast's wild eyes. An engine roared – just like a wild beast. The lights grew larger and larger and the roar grew louder. Something – a tractor, I think – some huge vehicle – was charging at us from the side.

The next second the bus was struck a powerful blow – a jarring, terrible blow. I heard the driver let out a ragged, guttural scream. The bus gave a stomach-turning heave under me and lifted up on to one side. For an endless moment, it hung there, balanced precariously on two of its tires.

Then all of us – me, the guard and the driver – shouted as the bus tipped over.

I was flung, tumbling, through the air, my shackles rattling. I smacked down hard against the edge of the seat across from me and fell hard and painfully against the metal grate of the far window.

Every light went out. I heard glass shattering, a crunch of

metal. Beneath the grinding roar of the attacking engine there came another sound: a series of short, sharp pops. The next moment, I smelled something sour and awful filling the bus.

I heard the guard shout, 'Tear gas!'

It filled the air in seconds, thick and smothering. I gasped for breath, trying to bring my chained hands up to cover my mouth, unable to reach it. I shut my eyes, but it was too late. My eyes burned as if they were in flames. Tears poured down my cheeks. I felt myself fading into unconsciousness as the gas grew thicker.

Then hands were clutching at me, clutching my arms. There were deep, harsh shouts all around me. A confusion of voices. I was hauled upright.

The next thing I knew, there was air – cold refreshing night air – flowing over me. I was moving through the downpour – half stumbling in the small steps that were all the shackles would allow – half dragged by the unseen people on either side of me, clutching my arms . . .

Then the scene was over, gone. It blew away like smoke. These memory attacks were like that. They were like dreams where time and place changed without warning.

I was in a car now. The shackles were gone. My hands and feet were free, but I could still feel the pressure of the fetters on my wrists as if they'd only just now been broken off me. There were people near me, bodies pressed close on either side. They smelled wet, sweaty, bad, and I smelled bad too. It was uncomfortably steamy and warm in the car and I could sense it was uncomfortably cold and damp outside.

'We're here,' said a gruff voice.

The car had stopped. From the back seat, I leaned forward to peer out through the windshield. Lightning struck and, in the flash, I saw a house, a mansion, standing on a little hill. It was a weird, spooky-looking place – an unforgettably bizarre building. It had a tall central tower in the middle with a lower tower on one side and an entryway beneath a pitched roof on the other. It had all kinds of frills and decorations, each a different shade of gray.

I didn't know how far we'd come from the bus. I sensed it was a long way. I didn't know what state I was in anymore. I didn't know where Waterman and Rose were or any of the other people who had come up with this insane idea to recruit a high-school student to infiltrate a terrorist cell. Did they know where I was? Were they even aware that any of this was happening?

In another flash of lightning, the crazy-looking house appeared again and sank again into darkness. I sensed that this was the crucial place, the crucial moment of the operation. This was the Homelanders' headquarters.

I would be welcomed here – or killed – one or the other.

It was suddenly day, just like that.

My orange prison jumper was gone and I was dressed in jeans and a black T-shirt. I was standing in a bedroom. The room looked like it had been decorated by some eccentric millionaire, with decorations so fancy they were almost comical. There were heavy purple drapes with gold fringes hanging in elaborate folds around the windows. There was a domed clock ticking away on a mantelpiece that was crowded with other smaller clocks, all of them ticking away. A fire was burning in a fireplace so large it could've housed a family of four. There were elegant antique wooden chairs and tables crowding the floor. And the bed – the bed was an enormous four-poster and was hung with drapes as thick and colorful as the ones on the window.

I knew I was inside the bizarre mansion, the house I'd seen last night. I knew I was in a room in one of the towers, probably the tall one in the center. I was about to go to the window to look out, to try to get my bearings. But, before I could, the door opened. A man was standing there. He was a young man, about my age, a little older. He was trim and handsome with floppy blond hair falling across his forehead. He had a machine gun cradled in his arms, its strap around one shoulder.

It was a strange double moment for me, a moment that seemed to exist in two separate times at once. I knew this man and yet I didn't know him. Here, in this memory, he was a stranger to me. I had never seen him before. But somehow inside my mind was the knowledge that his name was Orton. His name was Orton and he was going to die. Not now, but later, months from now. He was going to be shot right in front of me. He was going to fall dead at my feet.

'Let's go,' he said. He made a gesture with his head and

with his machine gun. He was strong, sure of himself. I wondered how he would feel, how he would behave, if he knew he only had months to live.

I followed him out of the room.

The dream – the vision – the memory, whatever it was – skipped a step. The next thing I knew, Orton was opening another door and showing me into another room. I stepped across the threshold and saw the man named Prince, the leader of the Homelanders.

Waterman had shown me his pictures, told me his history: a Saudi terrorist who made a habit of blowing up innocent civilians in England, in Israel and now here. I had the same weird feeling as with Orton, the same strange doubling. I'd never met the man in the flesh before and yet somehow I felt I already had. It was as if I was living back then and now at the same time.

Prince's office – assuming that's what this was – seemed to have been decorated by the same kook who'd decorated my bedroom. There were the same purple-and-gold drapes hanging everywhere, even in places where there seemed no purpose to them. There was an enormous window on one wall and an enormous mirror with a curving gilt frame on the wall across from it. The mirror reflected the blue sky and the sunny new day, making the whole room bright.

Beneath the mirror, there was another apartment-sized fireplace. There was a gilded writing desk and gilded chairs on a colorful rug. There were quaint little gold and porcelain knick-knacks cluttering just about every flat surface in the room.

But I didn't have time to look around much; Prince commanded my attention.

He was standing behind a mahogony desk that was approximately the size of Kansas. Even at a glance I could see he had a powerful, charismatic presence. He was in his thirties, I would guess. About medium height. He had dark skin and straight black hair and a neatly trimmed black goatee. His large brown eyes were bright with a ferocious intelligence. He was dressed all in black – black slacks, black shirt – and I thought nervously, *That's convenient, anyway. It's always easier to pick out the bad guys when they dress in black.*

He made an elegant gesture with one hand, pointing me to the gilded chair that stood before his desk. When he spoke, his English was perfect, but his accent was thick and smooth, sort of like syrup.

'Have a seat, Charlie,' he said.

Just in case I didn't get the point, Orton nudged me in the back with his machine gun. I saw a look of annoyance flash across Prince's face.

'That'll be all, Orton,' he said.

'Been great knowing you,' I added.

Orton smiled at me in a way that wasn't really smiling – the way a crocodile smiles at you just before he eats you for dinner. Then he backed out of the room, keeping his eyes on me the whole way. He pulled the door shut hard when he left.

Prince gestured to the chair again. I sat down.

'It seems Orton doesn't like you,' Prince said.

'Maybe he's just shy.'

Prince's teeth flashed white against his olive skin. 'Or maybe he thinks you can't be trusted.'

'Why would he think that?' I said, trying to sound calm.

Prince shrugged. 'Frankly, I think he's a little jealous. Perhaps he senses your potential. He's been our star pupil up till now.'

'Oh yeah?' I said. 'And now?'

'That remains to be seen, doesn't it?'

'I guess it does.'

All this meaningless back-and-forth – I guessed it was some kind of test. You know, to find out if I was nervous or hiding something. I tried to sound casual, but I could feel my heart beating rapidly. I mean, it wasn't like a quiz in school where, if you give the wrong answers, you get a bad grade. If Prince had even the slightest suspicion I was a double agent, I was pretty sure he would shoot me dead on the spot. Maybe that's why he had such a colorful rug: so the bloodstains wouldn't show.

Now Prince settled into the high-backed swivel chair behind his Kansas-sized desk. He brought his two hands together in front of him, bridging the fingers. He swiveled back and forth a little, studying me. 'You know who I am, don't you, Charlie?'

'I know *what* you are,' I said. I was trying not to seem

29

intimidated by him. I *was* intimidated by him, but I was trying not to seem like it.

'Your history teacher, Mr Sherman, has been telling you about me.'

'That's right.'

'And what has he told you?'

'He said you were a powerful guy with powerful ideas. He said, even if they convicted me of killing Alex, you could get me out of prison.'

He spread his hands, gesturing toward the room. 'As you see.'

I nodded. 'So far,' I said. I didn't want to give him too much too fast. During the course of my murder trial, Sherman had been telling me all about his friends, the Homelanders, all about what they were trying to do, and how I could join them and help them in their mission. I'd pretended to let him convince me slowly, but I couldn't seem to have changed too suddenly or completely. My life depended on making this convincing.

Prince now brought his hands back together and tapped his fingertips against each other thoughtfully. 'What else has Mr Sherman told you?'

'He told me you wanted to destroy my country.'

Prince laughed – or at least he flashed his white teeth again. 'That's a little strong. I don't want to destroy your country, Charlie. I just want to . . . transform it.'

I managed to smile back. 'Transform it; right; that's what I meant.'

Prince turned his chair a half cycle and stood up out of it. He walked across to the big window and looked out at a blue sky with large white clouds moving swiftly through it.

'Do you think your country is perfect?' he asked me.

'Obviously not, since it's sending me to prison when I didn't do anything. If I thought it was perfect, I wouldn't be here, would I?'

'Exactly. Exactly.' He stood silently looking out. Then he said, 'People don't like change, Charlie. They get set in their ways very easily. Custom – habit – is like a drug, very addictive. Before they're willing to embrace a new way, they have to be shaken up. They have to be . . .' He tried to find the word.

I helped him out. 'Terrorized,' I said.

'Frightened, yes. They have to understand that they can't hide from what's coming. That nothing can protect them from it.'

'Protect them from . . .'

'Righteousness,' he said. He turned to face me and I saw now that the brightness of his brown eyes was not intelligence – or, that is, it wasn't *just* intelligence. It was madness too. He was out of his mind with a mad dream of power. 'Nothing can protect them from righteousness,' he said. 'You believe in righteousness, don't you, Charlie? You believe in good and evil.'

'Sure,' I said.

'Your country is steeped in evil, in false religion, in false freedom that lets people choose to do what's wrong in the eyes of God. Take your own situation.'

'What about it?'

'Well, you said it yourself: Would a righteous nation allow you to be sent away to prison for twenty-five years for something you didn't do?'

I didn't answer him. I'd been listening to Sherman talk like this for weeks now. It was always the same. They start with a falsehood: *You think your country is perfect.* Then they disprove the falsehood: *Your country makes mistakes.* Then they leap to an even bigger falsehood: *Therefore, your country is evil.*

I knew what Sensei Mike would say: *What a bunch of chuckleheads!*

But I didn't say that. I didn't think it would be wise. I didn't think it was a good idea to try to explain the whole God-made-us-free-to-choose business either. I didn't try to tell him that that's why it's not a question of whether your country is perfect or imperfect, it's a question of whether it's free or not free. Somehow I just didn't think Prince would get any of that. And I didn't want to stain his pretty rug with my blood.

'So you're going to blow people up until they're righteous,' I said – but I smiled as I said it, as if I were joking.

Prince flashed those pearly teeth again, moving back to his chair. He stood behind it, his hands on the high back as he swiveled it, meditatively, this way and that.

'Something like that,' he said. 'Something very much like that, in fact. And the question is, are you going to help us? We'll have to doctor you up a little so you don't look too much like your wanted posters, but then, with a face like yours, with an all-American demeanor like yours, with your knowledge of the customs of the country, you could get into a lot of places I might not. You could help us a lot, Charlie, if you wanted to. Do you want to?'

I let a long moment go by, but there was never any question what my answer would be. Prince and I both knew he would kill me if I said no. He would kill me if I said yes and he didn't believe I meant it. But I had already told Sherman I would join the group. That's why they'd busted me out in the first place.

So I nodded quickly. 'Sure,' I said. 'Count me in.'

Chapter Five

The White Room

The moment I spoke those words, the scene seemed to melt away from around me. It was as if Prince and the fancy room and the strange house had all been sculpted out of ice and now the heat had risen under them and they were melting, pouring down into nothingness.

I heard a buzzer. A loud clanking sound . . . Suddenly I was back in Abingdon, back in my cell.

My heart sank as I realized where I was: on the cot, curled up on the thin mattress. My body ached and stung all over, not just from the beating I'd gotten from Dunbar but from the spasms of the memory attack. I felt as if someone had gone through my insides with a staple gun: not a great feeling, if you've never tried it.

I blinked into the present, dazed and confused. There was a dark form hanging over me. I squinted, trying to bring the form into focus. It took me a minute before I saw that it was a guard.

'Get up, West,' he commanded. 'You have a visitor.'

I blinked, licking my dry lips. I could barely understand what he was saying. 'A visitor . . . ?' I murmured hoarsely. 'Is it Saturday?'

'Get up!' he said again. He wasn't much of a conversationalist.

I uncurled my body slowly, each motion sending pain through the core of me.

'Come on, come on!' said the guard.

He gripped my arm and yanked me to my feet. The sudden movement sent a sharp pain shooting through my head. My hand went up and I felt the egg-sized bump there. That was where Dunbar had smacked me into the floor.

'Too bad about that fall you took,' the guard said, smirking.

'Yeah,' I said through my fingers. 'Next time, I'll watch where I'm going. Walked right into Dunbar's fist.'

The guard stopped smirking. 'I wouldn't mention that to anyone, if I were you. Not unless you want to go back to the Outbuilding.'

'Whatever,' I said. I tried to play it tough, but the very mention of the Outbuilding made me clutch with fear. 'Where's my visitor?'

He jerked his head toward the open door. 'Let's go.'

He herded me out of the cell and along the second tier of cells and down the stairs. We went past a Plexiglas module where a guard sat at a control desk surrounded by computers and security monitors. There was an iron door blocking the way ahead.

The guard with me nodded at the guard in the module. There was a loud buzz and the iron door slid open.

We went through the door and down a faceless concrete hallway. There were more doors: white doors in the white wall, almost invisible. We stopped in front of one of them. The guard unlocked it with a key and pulled it open. He tilted his head for me to go inside.

I stepped through and he slammed the door behind me. I heard the key turn again, locking me inside.

I looked around. There wasn't much to see. It was a small, cramped white room. There were no windows, no two-way mirrors, just the rough painted surface of the blank white cinder-block walls. There was a white table bolted to the floor and two plastic white chairs, one on either side.

For a minute or two, I just stood there, staring stupidly at all that whiteness. I was still a little messed up in my head. The memories from my attack still clung to me. The scene had been so real; it was so much as if I were there, right there. It hurt to be back here again, back in this prison. Anyplace would have been better.

I heard the lock on the white door snap again. The door opened.

I turned and saw Detective Rose step into the room.

Man, I can't tell you what that was like. At the sight of him, I felt my sore, battered body go weak with relief. I couldn't remember the last time I was so happy to see anyone.

'Rose!' I blurted out. 'Dude! Oh, man, it's about time you showed up!'

Rose didn't answer. His face was blank, expressionless. But then he never was much in the expressing-himself department. He was a black guy with a round face and flat features, a thin moustache and smart, steady eyes. He rarely smiled. He rarely even grimaced. Even his suits seemed to have no particular color. He was always all business.

I saw his eyes go over me, pausing on the cuts and bruises. But all he said was, 'Sit down, Charlie.'

I lowered myself painfully into one of the white chairs. Rose didn't sit down in the other one. He put his foot up on its seat. He rested his arm on his raised knee. He looked down at me – studied me – for a long time.

'What happened to you?'

'I fell down,' I said.

He snorted. 'You fell down, huh?'

'I fell down on a sadistic guard.'

'That *was* clumsy of you.'

'Tell me about it.' I looked up at him, searching his eyes for something, some kind of hope. I couldn't stand the suspense. 'So,' I said to him. 'Are you gonna get me out of here or what?'

'What's the matter, Charlie? Don't you like prison?'

I wanted to come up with a snappy answer, but I wasn't feeling very snappy. 'It's bad,' I admitted. 'I'm trying to stay strong in here, you know? But I'll tell you the truth, Rose: it's really, really bad.'

I thought I saw a trace of sympathy rise in Rose's eyes, but it was tough to tell. He just nodded. 'That's the way it works,

Charlie. You put a lot of bad guys together in the same place, you end up with a pretty bad place.'

'Are you talking about the inmates or the guards? Because in here, it's hard to tell the difference.'

The faintest trace of a smile appeared at one corner of Rose's mouth. 'The guards wear the blue shirts.'

I tried to laugh. I tried to sound hard and cool the way Rose did. But even I could hear the desperation in my own voice and I'm sure Rose could hear it too. The truth was I didn't know how much more Abingdon I could take.

'So?' I said again, my voice shaking a little. 'What's the deal? Are you gonna get me out of here?'

Rose let out a breath. Something about the way he did it made my stomach churn. I could feel the bad news coming.

He took his foot off the chair. He sat down across from me. He leaned forward, his elbows on the table, his eyes steady on mine.

'Here's what's been happening since they put you away in here,' he said. 'The Homelanders' organization has been broken. The men we arrested at your friend Margaret's house? They talked. They led us to their headquarters . . .'

'That crazy-looking mansion?'

'The crazy mansion, yeah. We've still got it under guard. They had computers there, papers, names, locations. Those led us to the training camp – the place you escaped from. A series of safe houses. We've rounded up almost all of them. The Homelanders are over. They're done.'

He let that sit for a minute between us, gave me time to take it in.

'So . . . that's good news, right?' I said finally. 'The operation was a success. I did what you wanted me to do. Hooray, right? America is safe. You get a promotion. Waterman can rest in peace. And, listen, as far as I'm concerned, you can forget my parade and the medals and all that. Just get me out of here and let me go home, OK?'

There was another moment of silence. Then Rose said the words that made my breath catch with fear.

'It's not that simple.'

'What do you mean?' I asked, my voice rising. 'What do you mean, it's not simple? Sure it's simple. It's really simple. You hold a . . . Whattaya call it . . . ? A press conference or something. You hold a press conference and you say, "Hey, remember the whole Charlie-West-is-a-murderer thing? Surprise! We were only kidding. He helped us bust up this terrorist ring and now we're gonna set him free so he can have his own reality TV show . . ." I don't care what you say, man. Just get me out of Abingdon before I—'

Rose interrupted me, speaking in the same flat voice with the same expressionless expression on his face. 'I can't.'

I was in the middle of a sentence when I felt the words turn to ashes in my mouth. 'What do you mean, you can't?'

'I'm sorry,' Rose said.

I swallowed, hard. 'You mean you can't get me out of here?'

'No.'

39

'Not ever?'

His eyes flicked away from mine. 'Not yet. Not now.'

I felt the strength go out of me. I sagged against the chair.

Rose went on speaking, without emotion. 'You knew the risk when you signed on, Charlie. Waterman's operation – our operation – it was never strictly . . . official. We never really had approval from our superiors. The government is happy to take the Homelanders into custody in a quiet way but, right now, they don't want it to go any further than that.'

'Any further than what? These people are terrorists. They're at war with us. Why should we tiptoe around about putting them in jail?'

Rose cupped his hands over his nose and mouth and closed his eyes, almost as if he were praying. But I think he was just trying to gather his thoughts, trying to figure out how he was going to explain this to me. I was pretty interested to hear what he'd come up with.

'Here's the deal,' he said finally, dropping his hands. 'An organization like the Homelanders doesn't just spring up out of nowhere. People fund it, plan it, support it. Powerful people in countries in the Middle East.'

'So?'

'We need help from some of those countries. Help with security. Help with arms negotiations. Help with oil.'

'Oil.'

'Right now, it's convenient for a lot of people in the government to pretend that the Homelanders were just a random bunch of crackpots. And that you were just a troublemaker who got involved with them. That way, there's no pressure from the people, from the media, to go too high up the ladder, to embarrass the people we need to deal with . . .'

Suddenly I found myself on my feet. The plastic chair toppled over behind me, rattling against the floor.

'Embarrass them?' I shouted. 'Embarrass them? They're just going to leave me to rot in here so they won't embarrass people in the countries where these killers came from?'

'It's a sensitive moment, Charlie. A very powerful faction in our government is too determined to believe the Homelanders didn't really exist at all—'

But I silenced him with a raised hand. I turned away from him. Paced to the wall. Braced my hands against it, my head hung down. I could barely believe what I was hearing – and, at the same time, I believed it too well.

Behind me, Rose said, 'There's something else you oughta know . . .'

I just stood there, head hanging, waiting for it.

'We didn't get them all.'

Now I swung around, looked at him, eyes glaring.

'Prince escaped,' he said.

'Prince . . .'

'And some of his top operatives – some portion of his operation – we don't know how much . . .'

'But Prince was the head guy. He was the brains behind the whole deal . . .'

'I know that.'

'Well, do you have any idea where he is?'

Rose looked down at his hands clasped together on the surface of the desk. He was silent for a long moment. Then he raised his expressionless face and stared at me with eyes that said more than he could say aloud. 'The government is convinced he's left the country.'

'Because they want to be convinced. Because it's convenient.'

He nodded.

'But what if he hasn't?' I said. 'What if he hasn't left?'

'Well,' said Rose. 'If he hasn't left . . . you may not be safe.'

I let out a laugh – if you can call it a laugh. 'Oh really? I'm not safe? What a surprise. I thought I was snug as a bug in a rug in here! I mean, it's not as if someone just tried to slice me to pieces. It's not like some guard just used me as a punching bag for half an hour.'

'Look, I'm working on this,' said Rose. 'I am. It's just . . . They've closed Waterman's operation down. I have no official power base anymore. I'm doing my best to go through channels, through friends . . .'

Angrily, I reached down and snapped up my chair. 'Channels!' I said. 'Friends!' I plunked the chair down across the table from him. I plunked myself down into it. I was so mad I hardly felt the aches in my body anymore. 'Let me see if I've got this right. Most of the Homelanders are in custody but the government doesn't want to admit they were a highly funded organization taken down by an unofficial undercover organization. Because of their negotiations in the Middle East, it's more convenient to pretend the whole thing is over – and to keep me in here, with everybody thinking I'm a murderer. Meanwhile, Prince has escaped and wants me dead but you have no way to find him because the government prefers to believe he's gone and you have no power base. So not only am I stuck in this hellhole, I'm a sitting duck for anyone who wants to earn Prince's favor by bumping me off. Have I got all that right?'

For the first time, Rose showed some sign of strain. He rubbed one eye wearily. It was a quick gesture, over in a moment, but it revealed to me how tired he was, how hard he'd been working on all this.

'You need to try to be patient—'

'Patient?' I slammed my fist down on the table. 'You don't know what it's like in here.'

'I understand, but—'

'What if I call the newspapers?' I said. 'What if I tell them about Waterman? About the Homelanders? About what went down? How it all happened?'

'Who do you think people will believe?' Rose asked quietly. 'A convicted murderer telling people he's secretly a hero who busted up a terrorist organization – or a lot of serious-looking officials in suits saying he's just one of a bunch of troublemakers?'

I didn't answer. I knew he was right. No one would believe me if I told the truth. Even I could hardly believe it. I buried my face in my hands. I don't think I'd ever felt so low, so helpless, in all my life.

'Listen,' Rose went on, 'I'm working on something, OK?'

It was another moment before I could look up. 'On what?'

'An appeal. Through your lawyer. In the courts. We've got friends there – people who know the truth. If they can arrange for the evidence against you to be declared tainted, your conviction could be overturned.'

'Overturned,' I said roughly. The word would hardly come out.

'I know. It's not a complete vindication but . . . at least it'd get you out of here.'

I looked at Rose – and, again, his eyes flitted away. He couldn't meet my gaze. He was ashamed of the position he was in, ashamed of what the government was doing to me. I didn't blame him. On the other hand, when Waterman first recruited me for this job, he didn't lie about it. He told me I was risking everything. Not just my life, but my reputation. He told me he was operating outside the usual channels. He told me I might not have the support of the fancy suits in government. He told me they might pretend I didn't exist and that the people I loved might go to their graves believing I was a traitor and even a killer.

I'd signed on, knowing all that. And I'd won, too. Me and Waterman and Rose and the others – we'd done what we set out to do. We'd broken up the Homelanders, stopped them – most of them, anyway – before they could carry out their plans. All except Prince and a few of his friends.

So I had nothing to complain about. I'd known what I was getting into from the start.

I just hadn't known about Abingdon – how hard it would be, how lonely and terrifying and suffocating. That's just not something you can know before you get there, before you experience it for yourself.

And now that I did know, I wasn't sure I had the courage to stick it out.

'How long?' I asked Rose hoarsely. 'How long would an appeal take?'

'With our friends working on it,' he said. 'A couple of months maybe. If all goes well, you'll be out of here early in the new year.'

I let out a long breath. 'Christmas in Abingdon,' I murmured. 'Just what I always dreamed of.'

'I'm sorry,' Rose said. He still wouldn't look at me.

Finally, after what seemed like a long silence, his chair scraped against the floor as he pushed it back. He stood up. He hesitated, standing over me.

'I'll tell you something, Charlie,' he said then. 'When you started this, you were a boy. But you're not a boy anymore. You're a man. A man and an American. And I don't say either of those things lightly. You're getting a hard deal from some people who aren't fit to tie your sneakers. Government can be like that. That's one of the reasons we try not to have too much of it.'

He moved away from me. He went to the white door in

the white wall. He rapped against it. Then he looked back at me over his shoulder.

'You won't be seeing me after this, Charlie. I won't be able to get in touch with you directly. But, believe me, I won't forget you. I'll be working on getting you out of here any way I can. And if there's any news, I'll find some way to let you know.'

The door opened. I could see the guard standing in the hall outside.

'How can I reach you?' I asked him.

He shook his head. 'You can't.'

'But . . .' I stared after him desperately. 'Who do I call if I need help?'

Another very slight trace of a smile touched the corner of his lips. 'You know how to pray, don't you?' he said.

And he walked out.

Chapter Six

Advent

Even in Abingdon, you could feel Christmas coming. There was something in the air – something, I mean, besides the usual tension, terror and rage. Each day, there were fewer fights in the yard. More cons started talking about visitors. Even people who never got visitors the rest of the year got visitors now. And there were Christmas cards in the mail. The prisoners taped them up on the walls of their cells as decorations.

The Salvation Army had a program called the Angel Tree. Cons were allowed to ask for presents for their kids. Then the Salvation Army would hang the requests like ornaments on trees in malls around the country. People could pick off an ornament and buy the present that was listed there. Then the Salvation Army would deliver the present to the convict's kids as a way of showing them God loved them. The prisoners liked that program. I could hear them talking to each other about what they'd asked for, what their kids would get. It gave them something to think about besides the endless days locked away in this hole.

For me, though, Christmas just made things harder. I couldn't stop thinking about my home, my mom and dad, my friends. I couldn't stop remembering the stuff we'd do at Christmas time. Nothing special, really; just the usual stuff; but when it's gone, when there's a wall and bars and a barbed-wire fence and gun turrets between you and a glass of eggnog and *A Christmas Carol*, on TV and your sister getting so excited Christmas Eve she has to go to her room with a headache and your mom worrying the tree will catch fire and the radio playing songs that you can't help liking even though they seem to have been recorded when dinosaurs walked the earth . . . When you're locked away, all those stupid, ordinary things seem pretty exceptional, pretty sweet, and you miss them like crazy.

But I guess I thought about stuff like that only about every other minute or so. In all my spare minutes, I still kept watch, knowing it was only a matter of time before someone else tried to kill me, knowing there was still no place for me to run or hide.

Saturday came. It was my first visiting day. My mom and dad were coming. Beth too. I was excited. Really excited. I paced up and down in my cell: a step and a half from the rear wall to the bars, then back again. The morning went by even more slowly than usual.

Finally, the guard came to fetch me. He brought me to a room with a long row of windows set in the cinder-block wall. There was a low wooden stool in front of each window. The windows were separated from each other by small metal dividers. Black telephones hung on the dividers. Words painted on the wall above the windows said, 'Keep your hands visible at all times.'

The guard led me to a stool in front of a window in the middle of the row. There was a convict to the left and another to the right of me. Both were talking through their phones to people on the other side of their windows. They leaned in close to the glass for privacy, but there wasn't much privacy to be had.

I sat and waited, looking out through the window at the room on the other side. I could see the entrance to a hallway out there. I thought about how someone could walk down that hallway and leave the prison. Free. Just like that. Someone, but not me.

A minute passed, then another. Then my mom and dad came into sight, walking toward me down the hall.

I expected to be happy to see them. And I was, I guess. But it made my heart hurt too. It made me hurt to see the way my mom looked, all tired, and red-eyed like she'd been crying – crying and crying without stopping for more than a year, ever since this nightmare began. My dad looked better, better than he'd looked before I was arrested, anyway, when I saw him talking on TV. Back then, he didn't know the truth. But now Beth and my friends had explained to them about the Homelanders and, even though they didn't know the whole story, they'd probably guessed a lot of it. I think, as long as my father thought I was just on the run, wanted for murder – well, that was kind of tough for him to take. But now that there was a reason behind it all, now he understood that I was fighting for the good guys – I think that was easier for him. My mom didn't care why I was here. She just wanted me safe at home. But Dad understood that sometimes the right thing to do is dangerous and you just have to do it anyway. I know he understood because he was the first one who taught it to me.

I picked up the phone on my side. My mom held the phone on their side. My dad pulled up an extra chair and sat beside Mom with his arm around her shoulders. They peered through the window at me. I felt like one of the animals in the zoo.

Mom tried to be brave, but it was hard for her to get the words out, especially when she got a look at the bruises on my face, all purple and yellow now.

'Oh my God,' she said, the tears starting. 'What happened to you?'

'I'm all right,' I told her. 'Don't worry about it.' I didn't want to lie, but I knew she didn't want to hear the truth either. And I only had to glance over at my father to see he understood what had happened.

'Are you sure you're OK?' Mom said. 'Did they let you see a doctor, at least?'

I almost laughed. *Doctor Fist*, I wanted to tell her. *They let me see Doctor Fist*. Instead, I changed the subject. 'Listen, I have some good news. My lawyer says there's a chance my case is going to be overturned on appeal. He says I could be out of here in a couple of months.' I tried to make it sound like a sure thing, even though I knew it wasn't.

'That's wonderful,' Mom said through her tears – but I could tell she didn't believe me. She was just trying to sound hopeful for my sake.

'Mom,' I said. 'Really. It's all right. It's going to be all right.'

'That's great,' she said bravely, but she was just pretending still, I could tell.

When my mom couldn't talk anymore, my dad lifted his hand up and pressed the palm flat on the divider. I put my hand up and pressed it to his. He looked at me through the plexiglas. He didn't say anything. He didn't say he was proud of me or that I was like a part of him and he was suffering right along with me. He didn't say that he threw a father's heart on the altar of heaven every night in the hope God would protect me, or that he sent a father's blessings into the bowels of this hell every day in the hope it would sustain me. He didn't say any of that, but somehow he said all of it – the way he'd always said it – without speaking a word – just by being there.

After a while, he lowered his hand and I lowered mine. My dad helped my mom to stand and they went out together, slowly.

A couple of moments passed. Then Beth came down the hall.

I read a poem in school once. I can't remember the name

of it, but the guy in the poem said that he was afraid he was going to die 'like a sick eagle looking at the sky.' I remembered that poem now because that's how I felt looking through the thick square of Plexiglas at Beth: like a sick eagle looking at the sky. She looked good. Beth always looked good. Pretty, with her hair curling around her smooth cheeks, and her blue eyes bright. She was wearing a yellow blouse and new jeans and they looked good on her too. But the thing about Beth that was hard to describe was just how nice she was, how kind she was, and how it showed in her face and in her eyes.

In here, in Abingdon, you came to understand that kindness is like freedom – you don't know how sweet it is until it's gone.

When she sat down, when she looked through the window, when she saw how banged up I was, her mouth got all tight and her eyes got watery, but she didn't cry. I could see her forcing herself not to cry. She didn't ask what happened to me either. She knew.

It was a moment before she could speak. She just sat there, looking at me through the glass, holding the phone to her ear. Then she just said, 'Are you all right, Charlie?'

'Yeah,' I said. 'It's fine, Beth. It's nothing. I miss you. That's the hard part. I miss everyone. That's the only thing that really hurts.'

Her eyes lingered doubtfully on my purple bruises. But she said, 'You're going to get out of here soon. I know it.'

'Good,' I said. 'Hold on to that. Don't lose hope. Talk to my mom. Don't let my mom lose hope. There's an appeal in the works. It's going to take a month or two, but it could get me out.'

'Do you really think so?' she said. Her voice cracked. When I heard it, my heart cracked too.

'We'll see,' I said. 'They're working on it. We'll see.'

Her eyes went over my face again. 'A month or two. You'll miss Christmas.'

'I know,' I said. 'It's gonna be all right, Beth. Don't worry.'

'OK.'

'That was really unconvincing.'

'I'm so scared for you, Charlie. Look at you. Why don't they keep you safe?'

I tried to smile. 'Think of it as a chance for me to practice my karate.'

It wasn't much of a joke, but she tried to smile back all the same. 'That reminds me,' she said. 'Sensei Mike says hello. You weren't allowed any more visitors this week so he said he'd wait till there was an opening, then he'd come see you. Josh, too, and Miler and Rick. They want to come too.' Her voice caught a little again, and again I could feel it inside me. But she swallowed her tears. 'Sorry,' she said. 'It just seems kind of awful, you know. When I think about it, it seems kind of awful that they can keep you in here when you haven't done anything. It seems awful they can tell you who you can see or who can visit you.'

'Yeah,' I said. 'They can tell you just about everything. Where to go, what to do, when to eat . . .'

I had to stop talking then. I bit my lip. I just sat there, looking out at her through the window. Like a sick eagle looking at the sky.

When the guard came to tell us visiting hours were over, I felt something plummet inside me, going down, down, down very fast. It would be another week before I saw anyone I loved again: a week in here, surrounded by walls and guns and angry men.

I watched Beth go down the hall with the other visitors. Just before she went out the door, she turned back and waved. It's hard to describe what it was like to see her go, to see my parents go. There was that plummeting feeling but also – well, in some ways – I was almost glad they were gone. I hated to have them see me here. In this gray uniform with a number on it. With guards pushing me around and telling me what I could and couldn't do. An animal in a cage.

I'll get out, I told myself. *Rose'll get me out. Two months, maybe three. I just need courage. I just have to survive.*

That's what I told myself.

But I was way wrong.

Chapter Seven

Desperate Measures

Dinner time.

The cafeteria was a big room with green cinder-block walls and metal ceilings. There were long shiny metal tables with benches bolted to the floor on either side. The prisoners moved in a line past the service counter. A gray line of gray men. Staff servers scooped some kind of meat on to our plates. Some kind of vegetables and potatoes too. Guards stood against the wall and watched us, sharp-eyed.

I thought back to the cafeteria in my high school. I thought about clowning around there with Josh and Miler and Rick. I thought about the first time I talked to Beth, how she wrote her phone number on my arm. It was only a little more than a year ago. It might as well have been a lifetime.

I carried my tray to a spot near the wall and sat down. I had to eat and keep watch at the same time. If someone was going to try to kill me again, this would be a good place to do it, guards or no.

So I ate and I watched. It wasn't exactly what you'd call a

relaxing meal. There were no relaxing meals in Abingdon.

After a couple of minutes had gone by, I noticed something strange. No one else was sitting down at my table. The benches around me were empty, as if the other prisoners were avoiding me. That made my adrenalin start flowing. It wasn't normal. It meant something was going on. Something was about to happen.

What did happen took me by surprise. My table started to fill up – and all the prisoners who were sitting down around me were guys I had seen out in the exercise yard around the weights. They were the guys with swastika tattoos – the ones who had come to my rescue when I'd been attacked. Suddenly, they were on every side of me. My hand, lifting my spoon from the tray to my mouth, froze and hovered in mid-air.

'Go on eating,' said the man to my right.

I knew him. Everybody in Abingdon knew him. His name was Joe Chubb. His nickname was Blade. He was the guy who'd knocked out the wolf-face man when he tried to kill me in the yard. He was the leader of the swastika boys: not a nice guy. He was in here for murder. He'd beat a man to death in a bar, just punched him in the head until he stopped breathing. It was easy to picture him doing something like that, too. He was a scary-looking dude, no question. Tall and wide with dirt-brown hair and a face that looked like someone had banged it out of a rock with a hammer. His skin was full of ridges and scars. Some of them were acne scars. Some of them were put there with weapons of one kind or another. He wore a close, pointed beard that gave him a devilish appearance. But the scariest thing about him was the look in his eyes. It was a kind of a distant, dreamy look, but not in a good way. He seemed to be dreaming something violent and evil. It seemed like that was a good dream for him, like he was enjoying it and maybe when he woke up, he'd try to make his dreams come true.

He spoke in a low murmur, a guttural purr. It made me think of a cat torturing a mouse to death and having a fine old time at it.

'Listen,' he said. 'We're on the move. We could use you.'

I just sort of blinked at him. I didn't understand what he meant.

'We're getting out of here,' he went on, under his breath.

'Out?' I said.

'Keep your voice down, punk.'

Then I understood: they were planning an escape.

'Are you crazy?' I started to say. And then I dropped my voice to a whisper and said it again. 'Are you crazy? That's impossible. You'll be killed.'

Blade shook his head. He smiled a dreamy smile. 'Nothing's impossible, punk. It's all set. Right after Christmas.'

I took a quick glance around to see if the guards were watching us. They stood with their backs against the wall, scanning the room, but none of them seemed to be paying particular attention to me and Blade.

I pretended to go on eating. 'What do you want with me?' I asked him out of the side of my mouth.

'We could use you,' he said again.

'Why?'

'I can't explain that now. This isn't the time or place. Just tell me: are you in or out?'

I didn't know what to say. Why would a guy like Blade come to me? I just sat there, staring stupidly.

'In or out,' Blade said again, more urgently this time. 'Which is it, punk?'

Finally, I managed to shake my head. 'I've got an appeal on. My lawyer says I could be free in a couple of months . . .'

'Listen, brainless, you don't have a couple of months,' Blade purred with an ugly sounding laugh. 'Your Islamist buddies haven't changed their plans; I have that solid. They still mean to put a shiv in you. You stick around and the only way you'll get out of here is in a box.'

I glanced at him. He wasn't kidding. I believed him, too. Blade was the sort of guy who knew things, heard things. All the information in the prison seemed to make its way to him eventually. If he said the Islamists were going to try to kill me again, it was pretty certain he was right. It made sense, too. With Prince on the loose, every Islamo-fascist in the prison would be looking to take a shot at me and earn his favor.

'We won't be around to protect you this time,' Blade told me. 'One way or another, we'll be gone.'

I nodded. I understood. But what difference did it make? Obviously there was no way I was getting myself involved in a prison break – especially not with this gang of Nazi nutbags. I would just have to try to stay alive in here the best I could until Rose got me out.

'Good luck,' I said to Blade.

'Your funeral,' he answered curtly.

Then he and his friends all got up at once. I was alone again at the long table.

I sat there, staring down at my tray. I felt strange and unfocused, as if I were underwater. *What was I supposed to do now?* I wondered. *Now that I knew there was going to be an escape? Should I tell someone? Should I warn the authorities? Or should I just keep my mouth shut?*

Man oh man, it can be hard to know what to do sometimes – what's right, what's wrong. It can be easy in theory, sitting around thinking about it, but hard in fact, in life. There could be no mistake about one thing: Blade and his guys were killers, every one of them. Those swastikas tattooed on their arms and foreheads: they weren't some accident or some fashion statement or something. They weren't like some kid wearing a picture of Che Guevara on his T-shirt because he doesn't understand Che was a stone Communist killer, or some girl wearing a Soviet hammer and sickle for a belt buckle because she doesn't know the Soviets murdered a hundred million people. That's just ignorance, just dopiness.

But when these guys put swastikas into their flesh, they meant it. They wanted to express all the hate that symbol holds, all the evil and murderous meanness. If they got out of this place, they'd be doing the same sort of violence and murder that got them in here to begin with.

So I couldn't let them escape, could I? I had to turn them

in. I had to. Didn't I? I couldn't just let them break out and get free to hurt people again.

But then . . .

Well, they had saved my life, hadn't they? I knew they only did it because they were racist lunatics. Basically, if a black guy wanted to kill me, they were going to protect me on general principles, just to prove they were bosses of the yard. But the fact remained: I'd be dead if it weren't for them. The idea of ratting them out to the Abingdon guards – who were almost as bad as the prisoners – didn't feel right. It felt dirty.

And, OK, just being honest, there was something else, too. A rat in Abingdon is a dead man. If anyone ever found out I'd gone to the authorities – and they definitely would find out; they definitely would – the word would spread fast. Every single prisoner in this place would want me dead then. Some of them would come after me even after I got out of prison. They'd come after my family, after the people I loved. I'd never be able to rest.

So that was the situation: I had to stop these guys from breaking out, but if I ratted on them, I'd have a target on my back for the rest of my life. That's the thing, the crazy, brain-rattling thing about a place like Abingdon: when you're in a world of evil, all your logic gets turned upside down. What's right feels wrong; what's wrong feels like your only choice.

I tried to think what Sensei Mike would do, what he'd tell me to do. He was a war hero, after all. He had a piece of titanium in his leg from the time he held off an attack by a hundred Taliban almost single handedly in Afghanistan. He wouldn't be afraid of Blade or the guards or anyone who might come for him.

I knew he'd want me to try to stop this escape – but how?

A buzzer sounded. Dinner time was over.

I got up off my bench. My head was throbbing as if my brain were overloaded. I moved to the garbage cans, emptied my tray and set it on the stack.

I looked around. I saw the swastika boys gathered in one corner of the room, murmuring to each other, eyeing me with suspicion. I saw some of the Islamist gang looking at me from another corner, waiting for their chance.

I couldn't join one and I couldn't hide from the other. It was as if the stone walls of this prison were closing in on me from every side.

I took a step toward the cafeteria door . . . and, suddenly, the room went white. A terrible pain shot through me.

The next few minutes changed everything.

Chapter Eight

The Great Death

In an instant, the cafeteria was gone. The prison was gone. The present was gone and I was in the past again.

I was in the woods. I was running. Trees rushed by me on every side. It was night. It was pitch black but somehow I could see. The trees and vines and bushes – all the tangled shapes of the forest – appeared a ghostly green against the darkness. I understood: I was wearing military-style night-vision goggles.

I looked down for a second as I ran. I saw I was holding a machine gun: an AK-47 – compact and deadly. I kept running. I knew I had to run even though I didn't know why. What was I running away from? What was I running toward? I didn't know.

Slowly I began to comprehend. The idea just seemed to form in my mind. I was outside the secret Homelander compound in the woods. I was being hunted, hunted like a deer, by Orton and some of the others. I had that double sense again of being in two times at once: I felt as if I knew what was going to happen next. I couldn't know because it hadn't happened yet, and yet I did.

What I knew was this: someone was about to shoot me.

Almost the same second the knowledge came to me, it happened.

As if out of nowhere, Orton stepped from the trees. He lifted his AK and pointed it straight at my chest. For a second, I saw his face through the night-vision goggles, bizarre and green. I saw *his* goggles bugging out of his face like an insect's eyes. I saw his mouth gaping in a savage smile of pleasure and triumph.

Questions flashed through my mind: How had he gotten around in front of me? Why was he trying to kill me? Weren't we on the same side?

There was no time to figure out the answers. I had to move. Now.

Just as Orton stepped into view, I came down on my right foot. I pushed off hard to the side at the same moment he opened fire.

I heard the cough of the AK. I felt the bullets pepper my side. The impact spun me around in mid-air. I tumbled downward and smacked into the earth with a bone-jarring thud. As I landed on my shoulder, I somehow managed to keep rolling, twisting – somersaulting, finally, off the forest path and into the low bushes. I heard the AK death rattle yet again. I felt the bullets whistling above my head, off to the right.

Then, before Orton could pull the trigger one more time, I sprang up fast on to my knees and fired back.

He wasn't ready for me. He'd obviously lost me in the low brush when I fell and rolled. His second round of gunfire had been aimed in the wrong direction and now he was turned to face the empty woods to my right.

But I knew where he was. I'd heard his gun. I popped up out of my cover with my gun leveled at his center. I didn't hesitate. I opened fire.

Even in the strange green light of the goggles, I saw the dark stain spread over the front of his fatigues. The smile vanished from his face in a look of shock. He staggered backward, his arms flailing. He sat down on the hard dirt of the forest path.

At that, a whistle blew.

A man stepped out of the surrounding forest, stripping his goggles off his face as he came. I knew him: Waylon. One of the cruellest and most murderous of the Homelanders' band. One day soon, Detective Rose was going to shoot him dead. But now here he was, large and very much alive.

I stood up slowly. I stretched, trying to ease the pain in my side where the bullets had smacked into me. I stripped off my goggles too, as I came forward. I glanced down and there was enough moonlight for me to see the dark red-brown stain that had spread from beneath my arm all the way down to my belt. It was blood-colored paint, of course. This was a training exercise. The bullets were paint pellets that exploded on impact. They hurt something wicked when they hit you, and I knew I'd be bruised all over tomorrow, but they didn't break the skin. There were no wounds, no blood.

Waylon reached out and pushed my arm away so he could get a good look at where the pellets had landed. I flinched at the pain.

'Not so bad. Not fatal,' he said gruffly. He had a deep voice with a heavy Middle-Eastern accent. He was big and thickly built. He had a large face with sagging folds behind his scruffy black beard. 'You live to fight another day,' he said. Then he turned to Orton. 'But you,' he said roughly. 'You are dead.'

Orton was slowly getting to his feet. I could see his face contorted in pain. He looked down at the stains covering the front of his shirt. The grimace of pain became a grimace of anger.

'This is stupid,' he protested to Waylon. He gestured at me. 'Look at him. With those wounds, he would never have been able to jump up that way. I'd have finished him off while he was lying there.'

Waylon took a long stride and stood in front of Orton, looking down at him. 'You're forgetting one thing,' he said. 'You cannot possibly say such a thing to me. Do you know why?'

'Why?' said Orton angrily.

'Because you're dead,' said Waylon.

With that, Waylon hit Orton in the face, shockingly fast, shockingly hard, his open palm smacking loudly against his cheek . . .

And, with that smack, the scene was gone – and the blow seemed to hit me in the face instead of Orton. Confused –

and taken completely by surprise – I was sent reeling backwards by the impact.

I tried to steady myself, to get my bearings, look around. Everything had suddenly changed. I wasn't in the woods anymore. I was standing on hard-packed dirt. There were faces on every side of me: faces twisted, mouths open. People were screaming roughly.

Orton was there. Orton's furious face was bobbing around in front of me.

We were fighting, he and I. It was another training exercise: self-defense. But it wasn't like sparring back home in the dojo. In the dojo, Sensei Mike taught his students that, even when we sparred against each other, we were teammates. We weren't trying to hurt each other. We were trying to make each other better. Here, now, in the Homelanders' training compound, I could tell by the way my face throbbed that Orton was not holding back. He was a trained fighter, just like I was. And he'd hit me full force in the face. He wasn't trying to make me better at all. He was just trying to bring me down.

The full situation started to come back to me, in that weird double way things did come back during these memory attacks. Orton hated me. He was used to being the top dog among the Homelander recruits and he was jealous of my success. He meant to punish me for it. He meant to prove he was still the best, even if I got hurt in the process. Even if I got killed in the process.

He closed in on me again. His stare was intense, focused. His features were taut with purpose, his mouth twisted in a fury for revenge. I could hear the crowd of men around us cheering for him fiercely. I could see their bared teeth, their gleaming eyes on every side of me.

With no wind-up, no warning, Orton launched a high crescent kick. The edge of his foot came looping toward the side of my head. I was still dazed from his last punch. I only just managed to duck the blow. His sneaker swung past, above me, but he was already using the velocity of the kick to bring himself spinning full around like a top, his hand snapping out in order to send a chop at my neck.

I managed to get an elbow up, fending off the worst of the strike. But I was off-balance. The movement sent me stumbling to the side, tumbling to the ground as the crowd cheered with bloodlust. I rolled on to my back and Orton, still moving, flung himself at me. I lifted my feet and caught him in the belly and somersaulted backwards. The throw sent him flying through the air.

I got up as he hit the ground. I saw dust puff up all around him. I heard the breath come out of him with a loud grunt. I rushed to attack him before he could stand, but he was too quick. He rolled to the side and was on his feet before I could reach him.

The crowd moved with us, leaving us just enough space to fight as they pumped their fists at us and cheered.

Orton and I circled each other. He was good, tough, fast. And I could see by that angry gleam in his eye that he didn't mean to lose to me ever again.

As for me, I was out of breath, dazed from the blow to my

face, aching all over. I wasn't sure I could handle another solid attack.

Fortunately, before Orton could make his next move, Waylon stepped in between us.

He was even more frightening by daylight: big and ruthless with nothing but meanness in those baggy eyes.

'All right,' he said in his guttural accent. 'That's enough.'

I put my guard down. I breathed a sigh of relief. I was pretty sure I'd gotten out of a very bad situation there. If Orton had attacked again, he probably would've finished me off.

Waylon turned to Orton. 'Good job,' he said.

Then he kicked me in the chest.

It was a back-kick, perfectly planted. It hit me right above the heart. I went flying backwards and then dropped down to the ground, coughing.

Waylon turned and stood over me. 'You,' he said in his thick accent. 'You need to fight like you mean it. You are not in the dojo at the mall now. If you lose here, you die. You need to fight to kill.'

I started to get off the ground, but then . . .

. . . it was as if someone poured a giant glass of liquid night down over us. Darkness ran down on top of us and the training ground vanished . . .

I was suddenly in a silent hallway. It was dark, very dark. Even before I fully understood where I was, I knew I was in terrible danger. If anyone found me here, I'd be killed on the spot.

I pressed close to the wall. There was an opening up ahead: a doorway. I could make out the rectangle of moonlit night, lighter than the inner dark. I edged closer to the door. I peeked out.

From here, I could see the buildings of the training compound, hulking barracks and watchtowers surrounded by a high barbed-wire fence and the deep black expanse of the forest beyond. The structures of the compound were sunk in the night shadows – with one exception. One building, just across the way, over by the fence, had a yellow light burning in its window. A Jeep was parked outside.

It all came back to me now. I'd been in bed in the barracks. The other trainees were in bunks all around me. I'd heard the Jeep come into the compound. I'd heard voices calling to the guards to open the gates, tires on dirt, the car engine coming to a stop. Then there had been low voices – greetings and conversation.

I had looked around me to make sure the other trainees were asleep. Then I had gotten quietly out of bed to see what was happening.

That's why I was out in the hall wearing only sweat pants and a T-shirt. My feet were bare. I could feel the splintery wooden floorboards under them.

Prince.

That was the next thought that came back to me. It was Prince who had been in the Jeep. I'd recognized his voice out in the night. That's why I'd gotten up to take a look. That's why I was risking getting caught, getting shot.

Getting shot, I knew, was a serious possibility. Shifting my attention, I could see now that there was a guard in the watchtower to my left and another in the tower to my right. Both were holding high-powered rifles. There were two other guards standing together by the lighted building just across from me. I could hear these two guards speaking to each other in low murmurs. I had no way of knowing if there were other guards moving around in the compound's shadows, but I guessed there probably were.

Still, this was why I was here in the first place. This was what Waterman and his people had sent me to do: get information. Find out what the Homelanders were up to. Get the word out. Stop them before the killing started.

The guards outside the lighted building finished their conversation. They moved away from each other and walked off in opposite directions to begin their patrols of the area. Each guard carried an AK strapped over his shoulder.

The moment I saw them walk away from the lighted building, I started moving.

Crouching low, I took the last steps down the barracks hall to the doorway. I slipped outside, feeling the cool of the night surround me. The moon was just a sliver but it hung above the far trees and angled in across the open space of the compound, giving it some light. In that light, I could see the watchtower guards in silhouette, see they were turned to face out of the compound, watching for intruders from the surrounding woods. The two other guards, the ones on the ground, continued moving away, one off to my left, the other to my right.

I kept my head down and moved as quickly as I could across the open space. I took long, swift strides, careful my bare feet made no noise as they landed on the dirt. I headed for the lighted building.

That crossing – from my barracks to the building opposite – I guess it took maybe five seconds, all told: five terrible seconds when I was completely exposed. If one of the patrolling guards had heard me – if one of the watchtower guards had looked down and seen me – they'd have opened fire and shot me where I stood.

Then – thankfully – I was there. Panting, I came up against the lighted building. I pressed hard against the outer wall, trying to stay hidden in the shadows. The light within the building shone out through the window, falling on the dirt below, just inches from my feet. But the moon was still low enough to leave a line of darkness at the base of the building. I tried to stay inside that narrow line, out of sight.

From where I was, I could hear the burr of voices inside. It sounded as if there were two or three people in there. I strained my ears, listening. It was no good. I couldn't make out their words. I had to get closer.

I took a breath. I took a glance over my shoulder. I could see one of the compound guards. He was still walking away, but he was getting close to the furthest buildings over by the barbed-wire fence, under the watchtower. I figured, when he got there, he'd probably turn around and come back, heading straight toward me.

I turned to look for the other guard. He was gone. I scanned the night desperately. No sign of him. Where was he? Had he gone inside? Was he moving around to surprise me? I just didn't know – and there was no time to find out.

Just then, I heard the murmur of voices inside the building rise in volume.

'We don't have any choice,' someone said forcefully. I recognized the voice. It was Prince. 'We have to strike when we can, as we can.'

I stopped searching for the second guard. Time was short and I had to find out what was going on inside that room. I sidled closer to the window, my bare feet edging into that yellow glow of lamplight that fell on the dirt from inside.

I pressed hard to the wall and listened.

A voice spoke. It was Waylon, but he was talking in a quick guttural language I couldn't understand: Arabic, I guess. He spoke for several seconds.

Then a new voice interupted. 'Speak English, will you? I can't understand.'

I almost gasped out loud. I recognized that voice too. It was Mr Sherman, my history teacher. Even though I knew he was one of the Homelanders, I was shocked to find out he was here at the compound.

Waylon spoke again, in English this time. 'I'm telling you, it's too soon. He just isn't ready.'

Prince responded. It was the same calm, intelligent voice I remembered from the weird mansion. 'It doesn't matter,' he said. 'The simple fact is, we won't get another chance like this. Yarrow is the key to President Spender's new policy on terrorism. He's the one who's convinced the President to stand up to congress and declare a real homeland war against us. Killing him will throw their entire new security plan into disarray. After that, we'll be able to operate with a much freer hand.'

'I understand,' Waylon answered. I could hear him controlling his anger, afraid to challenge Prince. 'But the risk is too great. Charlie West is the most valuable asset we've ever acquired . . .'

At that, Mr Sherman broke in, giving a short laugh. 'There you go. I told you, Prince. I told you he was—'

'Quiet,' said Prince curtly.

That shut Sherman up. It was the only good thing Prince ever did. Made me wish I could have brought him to history class.

'No one ever doubted West was a fighter,' Prince went on quietly. 'It was his trustworthiness that was at issue. That *is* at issue still. Go on,' he finished – talking to Waylon, I guessed.

And Waylon did go on. 'I'm not a hundred per cent sure yet that we can trust West,' he said. I could imagine him staring pointedly at Sherman there. 'But I am a hundred per cent sure of this: the boy is a natural fighter. He's fearless. And, more than that, I have the sense you could put a hundred bullets in him and he would still get up, still try to bring you down. Assuming he can be trusted, that makes him one of our most important assets. It isn't worth risking him on a mission that hasn't been fully prepared.'

There was a pause. Once again, I took a quick glance at the guard behind me. He had reached the end of the compound now. He had paused by the far buildings, under the watchtower. He stood there, scanning the darkness. He would turn and start back my way any minute.

I looked in the other direction. I still couldn't find that second guard.

'It's prepared enough,' I heard Prince say then. 'We knew this was a possibility. Both West and Orton have been taught about that area just in case this contingency arose. They both know the bridge well.'

'As a training exercise. They don't—'

'And another thing: once West pulls off the assasination, we'll know we can trust him. Once he's killed for us, he's ours for good.'

'But he isn't fully—'

'No,' Prince cut Waylon off with finality. 'It doesn't matter. They're all expendable anyway. All of them. That's why we use them first: because it doesn't matter if they die. If we use them properly, without fear, we can show our enemies that we can do anything, get in anywhere, hit them in any way we want, while they can't even begin to find our center. West will assassinate Yarrow and if he's killed, he's killed. I appreciate your maternal concern for your trainees,' he said, his voice thick with sarcasm, 'but they'll all die eventually, Waylon. That's what they're for.'

Man! I thought. *I guess this is why they call him Prince. He's such a prince of a guy!*

Then Prince said, 'In the end, their purpose is simply to prepare the way for the Great Death.'

I heard a footstep behind me. I turned to see that the guard had started walking back across the compound, back my way. It would only be a few seconds before he would be close enough to see me pressed there against the wall, my figure outlined by the glow from the light inside.

But I couldn't escape. I couldn't leave. The Great Death? I had to find out what it was. It didn't sound good, that's for sure.

I pressed against the building again, listening.

'West and Orton – they're part of that plan too, though,' Waylon answered. 'That's their ultimate purpose.'

'Yes,' said Prince. 'But even if we lose them, even if we lose all of them, even if I have to do it on my own, the Great Death will not be stopped. The basic elements are already in place. Come what may, it will ring in the devil's new year. I will make sure of it personally, if I have to.'

I glanced over my shoulder. The guard kept coming toward me.

'What do you mean, "everything is in place"?' Sherman asked.

'It will be.'

'What about the CO device?'

'It's being acquired from the Russians. The arrangements are progressing.'

'When? When will we have it?'

'Soon.'

'How much?'

'Six canisters.'

'Six . . .'

'It's more than enough. Six canisters can be carried by a single man. So nothing will stop it, even if it comes down to me alone.'

I heard Waylon let out what must have been a curse in a foreign language.

I wanted to hear more – needed to hear more. But I was out of time. I had to get back to my barracks. Even now, the guard might see me sprinting across the open space.

I turned to move away from the building.

But before I could, a hand grabbed me by the shoulder.

Chapter Nine

The Infirmary

I opened my eyes and it was all gone: the compound, the buildings, the guards, all of it. No, wait. There was still that hand. It was still gripping my shoulder.

I turned my head, confused. Yes, there it was – that hand – powerful fingers digging painfully into my flesh.

I lifted my eyes and found myself looking up into the sadistic face of Chuck Dunbar, the Yard King.

'Wake up, garbage,' he snarled.

Fear shot through my confusion, bringing me fully alert. Where was I? What was happening? I tried to think. I remembered . . .

The cafeteria. Dinner. The swastika boys. Their plan to escape . . .

I'd had another memory attack. I'd collapsed on to the floor in pain. That meant that now I must be . . .

I looked around. Yes, I was in the infirmary. It was a narrow cinder-block rectangle of a room, the walls painted hospital green. There was a row of narrow cots lined up against one wall. There were prisoners in two of the other cots. The rest were empty. There was an observation window on the far wall at the end of the room. The window was empty, too: there was no one in the observation booth. The other sick prisoners had purposely turned their heads so they weren't looking at me.

No one was looking at me. No one was watching – which was exactly how Dunbar liked it.

The Yard King stood over my bed, gripping me hard by the shoulder. He sneered down at me, his eyes bright with malice.

'What do you want?' I said. My voice was thick and muddy.

With his free hand, Dunbar reached down and grabbed the front of my shirt. He yanked me up off the mattress. He stuck his face in close to mine. I could smell his dinner on his breath: dinner and beer.

'Why are you here?' he said in that raking-gravel voice of his. 'Why are you in the infirmary?'

'What do you mean? What . . . ?'

He shook me hard. I stopped talking. 'Have you got some kind of problem? Did you get hurt somewhere?'

'No, I—'

'I wouldn't like to think you got hurt in my yard, West,' Dunbar rasped. 'I wouldn't like to think you were telling people you got hurt in my Outbuilding.'

Now I understood. He was afraid I'd come here to talk, to inform on him, to tell someone how he'd roughed me up.

'Get your hands off me,' I said, grabbing at his wrist.

'Or you'll do what?' said Dunbar – but, all the same, he threw me roughly back down on to the cot.

I rubbed my hand over my face, trying to get my bearings, trying to de-fog my mind. My thoughts still seemed to be drifting in some weird netherworld between the present and the past.

'Come on,' Dunbar said. 'What did you tell them?'

'Listen—' I began.

He hit me in the side of the head with his open hand.

'Don't waste my time, West. Let's go! What did you tell them?'

I looked up at that nasty, knuckly face. I didn't like getting hit. I didn't like that he could just whack me like that and get away with it. He was a bully, that's all. A bully who knew he had all the power as long as we were here, as long as we were stuck together in the hell of Abingdon.

I couldn't keep the scorn out of my voice. 'I didn't come here to turn you in, Dunbar.' Slowly, painfully, I sat up on the bed. 'You don't have to be such a coward . . .'

That got to him. The truth always gets to guys like him. He grabbed me again, twisting the front of my shirt in his fingers as he hauled me to my feet, holding me close to his angry eyes. 'You listen to me, West. You open your mouth one time – one time – and, so help me, they will find your broken body—'

'I said get off me!'

I was too angry to stop myself. I knocked his hand away again. I staggered backwards as he let me go.

Dunbar looked surprised – surprised I dared to stand up to him, surprised that any prisoner would dare. But he smiled as I glared at him.

'Careful, West,' he said, very softly, very dangerously.

'Listen,' I told him. 'The next time you have me in your lousy Outbuilding, with your guards waiting out in the yard to help you so I can't fight back – then you can beat on me all you want. But you lay your hand on me in here again and you'll be in the infirmary with me.'

The bully's eyes widened in shock, then narrowed in rage. I was pretty sure no prisoner had ever talked to him like that before.

'Oh, you're gonna be sorry you mouthed off to me, garbage,' he said. 'Remember I told you I'm gonna make teaching you a lesson my hobby?'

'I remember.'

'Well, forget that. I'm gonna make it my profession. You think you have some kind of protection against me. You got no protection against me. When I decide to come for you, no one'll see, no one'll know, no one'll say a word. You'll just be gone.'

With that, he grinned – and turned to walk away.

I was glad to see him go. But before he reached the door, something happened.

It was like another memory attack – that harsh, that sudden, that real – but it only lasted a single second. One flash. One memory. That moment, out in the darkness, out in the shadows of the Homelanders' compound as I listened to the voices inside the building – I remembered Prince's voice . . .

The Great Death!

'Dunbar!' I called out. The word sprang from my mouth before I even had time to think about it.

The Yard King stopped about two steps away from the infirmary door. Slowly, he turned back to face me.

'You say something, garbage?'

I was about to answer when there it was again. The flash of memory. The night. The compound. The voices inside. The images and words rushed in on me too quickly for me to understand them all. But one thought stood out from all the others like a phrase written in fire in a paragraph of faded print.

The Great Death will not be stopped. It will ring in the devil's new year.

'I have to see the Warden,' I said softly, more to myself than to Dunbar. 'I have to talk to the Warden right away, right now.'

Dunbar narrowed his eyes. He pointed a finger at me. 'Just how short a life are you looking to have, you dumb—?'

'No,' I said. 'No, it's not about you. It has nothing to do with you. Listen to me, Dunbar. Something terrible is going to happen.'

I stood and stared down at the floor as the thoughts, the images, the memories kept flashing around me, engulfing me.

The Great Death will not be stopped . . . Even if I have to do it on my own, the Great Death will not be stopped.

It was hard to think straight but I knew I had to. I had to put the pieces together. Prince had escaped; Rose had told me that. Most of the Homelanders had been rounded up, but Prince and some of his accomplices were still at large.

Even if I have to do it on my own . . .

Rose's bosses in Washington were wrong. Prince hadn't left the country. The threat of the Homelanders wasn't over. As long as Prince was alive, as long as he was free . . .

The Great Death will not be stopped.

. . . he would somehow make sure the Great Death would happen. Whatever the Great Death was, Prince would see it through, even if he had to do it alone.

I had to tell someone, warn someone. But who could I tell? Who could I warn? How could I get the word out? In here. Stuck in here. Rose was gone. He said I wouldn't be able to get in touch with him anymore. Who else would believe me? My parents – my friends – maybe even my lawyers – sure. But none of them had the power to stand in the way of the Homelanders' plan.

The Great Death . . . will ring in the devil's new year.

New Year's: it was right around the corner, a little more than a week away. Whatever Prince was planning, there wasn't a lot of time to stop him. I had to think of something.

I raised my head slowly. I looked up at Dunbar. 'I need to talk to the Warden,' I said again. 'You gotta tell him, Dunbar. You gotta let him know. There's going to be a terrorist attack.'

'What?' said the Yard King, his rattling voice cracking with disbelief.

I stared up at him, hoping he could read the seriousness in my eyes, praying he'd believe me. 'People are going to die, Dunbar – a lot of people. You have to get me to the Warden. I have to tell him. I have to tell someone.'

Dunbar let out a harsh laugh. 'Man, you are one crazy—'

The next moment I was on him. I didn't think about it, I just leapt off the bed. One hand grabbed Dunbar's shirt, the other was on his throat, curved into a claw around his Adam's apple. I knocked him back against the wall and held him there, my eyes inches from his.

'Do it, Dunbar!'

He stared at me, his mouth open. 'Are you out of your—?'

'Do it,' I said. 'Or, so help me, I will turn you in for the things you do. Even if you kill me for it, Dunbar, I will turn you in and they will put you away. How do you think that'll be, huh? How do you think you'll do in prison? How do you think the cons'll treat you, once you're here on the inside?'

His eyes turned into deep pools of fear.

I clutched his throat tighter until he gagged.

'Get me to the Warden!' I said. 'Do it!'

Chapter Ten

The Warden

The Warden's name was Wilson Tanker. He was a large, square-built man with a shaven head and a sharp silver moustache. He wore a black suit and a black shirt and a string tie with a turquoise clasp. He had such narrow eyes they were almost buried in the wind-burned ridges and wrinkles of his cheeks. He seemed constantly to be squinting at you, like he was trying to make you out in the dark.

He was sitting in a swivel chair behind a gunmetal desk. It was daylight now; it had taken me more than twelve hours to get in to see him. The window behind him looked out on a section of the prison I'd never seen: a wall of grated windows across a narrow courtyard two stories down. Trucks occasionally rumbled through the court on their way from somewhere to somewhere else – somewhere I couldn't go.

There were two flagpoles against the paneled wall – an American flag and a state flag – one on either side of the window, on either side of Tanker as he leaned back and swiveled this way and that.

He had me standing in front of the desk. There was a guard standing beside my left shoulder and another standing beside my right. Chuck Dunbar was standing behind me. I guess you could say I was well guarded.

For a long time, Warden Tanker just went on swiveling back and forth, back and forth, squinting narrowly up at me.

Then after a while he said, 'And just how would you know there's going to be a terrorist attack on New Year's Eve?'

My frustration felt like a creature trapped in my chest trying to get out, a great big gorilla or something pounding on the cage bars of my insides. I let out a slow breath, hoping to calm the gorilla down. It didn't help much. 'I was with them,' I said. 'The terrorists. I overheard them talking.'

Warden Tanker looked at the guard to the left of me. Then he looked to the guard to the right of me. Then he looked over my shoulder at Dunbar. 'Uh huh,' he said finally. He had a thin reedy voice that came out of him in a slow drawl. 'So why did you wait until now to tell me?'

I stammered stupidly as I tried to put the words together. Finally, I managed to say, 'I didn't remember.'

Warden Tanker sort of rolled that around in his mouth for a moment, then drawled it slowly back at me: 'You didn't remember.'

'That's right!'

'Just kind of slipped your mind, did it?'

'Yes . . . No . . . I had amnesia.'

'Amnesia.'

'Well, not exactly amnesia. I took a drug . . .'

'I'll just bet you did.'

'No, not that kind of drug. A special drug so I wouldn't remember. So the terrorists couldn't get any information out of me.'

Once again, the gorilla of frustration threatened to tear me wide open as the Warden swiveled slowly, moving his eyes from one guard to another as if they were all sharing a private joke.

'And you got this drug exactly where?' Tanker asked. 'From the Amnesia Fairy, I'm guessing.'

The guard at my left shoulder snorted.

'Look,' I said, trying to control my temper. 'I know this all sounds hard to believe.'

'Oh, you know that, do you?' said the Warden.

'Yes, but you *have* to believe it. You *have* to.'

Slowly, thoughtfully, Warden Tanker stroked his silver moustache with his hand. The way he did it reminded me of Sensei Mike. Sensei Mike had a big black moustache and he'd stroke it with his hand sometimes when he was trying to hide the fact that he was laughing. But then Sensei Mike was always laughing because he thought the world was kind of a funny place in a lot of ways. The Warden, on the other hand, was laughing at me. 'Supposing I do believe you,' he went on – slowly. 'What do you expect me to do about it?'

The Frustration Creature was going so crazy inside me that, for a minute, I couldn't answer – couldn't answer without trying to throw this guy out the window. But finally, I managed to blurt out, 'Tell somebody! Homeland Security. The FBI. Anybody! What's wrong with you?'

I felt a sharp blow to the back of my head. I stumbled forward a step. Dunbar had hit me.

'Speak to the Warden with respect,' he growled.

'You see, son,' the Warden said – and I so wanted to punch him – 'my problem is, a lot of cons come in here with a lot of stories, hoping to get some new privileges or just start some kind of trouble. You know how I can tell when they're lying?'

I couldn't answer. I gestured helplessly.

'I can tell they're lying because their mouths are moving.' He waved me away like I was a bad smell. 'You have something you want to communicate with the outside world, call your lawyer.'

The guards on either side of me took hold of my arms, ready to drag me out of there.

'I *did* call my lawyer,' I said, as the Frustration Creature raged and hammered at the bars of his cage inside my chest. 'His office is closed for the holidays. Even if they get back to me – and even if they believe me – it could be too late.'

But the Warden wasn't listening. He had already opened a folder on his desk, was already turning to other business. 'Well, then I guess you're out of luck,' he drawled.

I started to answer . . . but then I stopped. My mouth shut with an audible sound. Because there was no point. The guards were drawing me toward the door and I realized there was no way I would ever make Warden Tanker believe me.

To him, I was just another lying con like a million others he'd seen. And the truth – the really terrible truth – was the story was so incredible, I'm not sure *I* would have believed me if I was sitting in his place.

'Come on,' said Dunbar, with a jerk of his head.

The guards pulled me toward the door. The Warden went about his business. And, as I stumbled out, it hit me full force: the Great Death was coming, coming soon, New Year's Eve.

And at that moment, suddenly – terribly – I knew what I had to do.

Chapter Eleven

One and a Half Steps

I paced my cell. A step and a half in one direction, a step and a half back. Again and again. Again and again. All the while, the Frustration Creature inside me stamped and raged, a beast in a cage of his own. But I just went on pacing. Back and forth. Back and forth. A step and a half. Again and again.

My thoughts were wild, out of control. It was like some kind of crazed conversation of gibbering voices all talking over each other and interrupting each other inside my brain. I was trying to think of some way out of this, a way other than the one that had come to me in the Warden's office – some way I could get the word out to someone who counted, warn someone who might be able to stop Prince, to stop the Great Death.

But who was there? It couldn't just be anyone. It couldn't just be a friend, or even one of my parents. How would that help? Who would they go to? Who would believe them? By the time they could reach anyone, convince anyone, it would be too late. There was so little time. No time, really. No details the police could work on, no proof, no way to know what the attack would be or even where it was going to take place unless . . .

Unless somehow I remembered. If I had ever known the answer, if it was still somewhere inside my mind, it might come back to me in the next memory attack. Or the one after that. It might . . .

But then what? Without Rose, without being able to contact Rose or anyone else who knew my mission, it still seemed impossible that I could catch up with Prince before he did whatever it was he was planning to do. There seemed no way. No way except . . .

Out of all those voices gibbering and interrupting in my brain, one kept speaking out louder than the others; one thought kept coming back to me: *If I were free* . . .

If I were free, I thought, I could do something. I could find my way back to the mansion, maybe, that crazy gray mansion sitting on the hill, the house Prince had used for his headquarters. It wouldn't be easy to find. I wasn't sure where it was. But I knew the location was in my head somewhere and I felt certain that, if I were free, I would be able to retrace my steps and get there.

If I were free . . .

I remembered Rose had told me that the mansion was still under guard and that it contained computers and records that had helped him and his agents arrest the other Homelanders. Maybe those computers and records held the key to where the Great Death attack was going to take place. Even if they didn't, if I could reach the mansion, I would also reach the guards around the mansion. I would be able to give them the word, warn them about the coming of the Great Death.

If I were free . . .

But there was no way to get free, no way to get out of this hell of a prison. Even if my lawyers did everything they said they would, even if everything worked out the way Rose hoped it might, there was no way I could get out of Abingdon in time.

No way, that is, but one. One insane, dangerous and totally desperate way.

I paced the cell. I paced the cell. One and a half steps back and forth. Again and again and again.

If I were free . . . If only I were free . . .

Then, finally, came what I was waiting for: the door buzzed, slid open. A guard shouted at our tier of cells: 'Yard time!'

Chapter Twelve

Blade

I stepped out into the yard. The sky hung low, dark gray and heavy. It seemed to press down on me. The cold air felt full of a coming storm.

I felt the danger on every side. Wherever I turned, someone was watching me, waiting for his chance.

Out by the basketball court, it was the Islamist crew. They were gathered at the edge of the black asphalt. They were stealing glances at me with deep, angry eyes, then turning away to murmur to each other.

Over by the Outbuilding, it was the guards. They were standing with Dunbar at the Outbuilding door. Dunbar lifted his chin in my direction, his face like stone. It was his way of saying, *I'm waiting for you, punk. I'm waiting for my moment.*

Then there were the musclemen over by the weights, the guys with the swastika tattoos. Blade was at the center of them, lying on a bench pressing about a gazillion pounds of weights on a bar. One of his buds noticed me and said a word

92

to him. Blade let the weights settle into the holder. Then he sat up on the bench and looked at me – not an angry look, but not a friendly one either. Kind of suspicious, I guess you'd call it. Like he was trying to take my measure, trying to figure out exactly who I was and what I was up to.

I started moving toward him.

It felt like a long way across the yard. The whole time I was walking, I felt all those eyes on me. The guards' eyes and the Islamists' eyes and the Nazis' eyes, too. As I came near the weight area, Blade stood up from the bench. He made a sort of ironic gesture, a sort of 'right-this-way' wave of his hand, letting me have a chance at that bar with its gazillion pounds of weights on either end.

I figured this was some kind of challenge, some kind of way for me to prove myself to these thugs, so I didn't hesitate. I lay down on the bench. I placed my hands on the bar. I took a breath and went for it. I strained as hard as I could, the breath coming between my tight lips in puffing grunts. I pushed and pushed against the bar, trying to lift it even an inch off its resting place.

No way. I might as well have tried to shift the moon.

I gave a gasp and my arms fell back.

Blade bent down and leaned his scarred, goateed face in close to mine, giving me a full look at his dreamy and murderous eyes.

'What's the matter, brother? Ain't you got what it takes?'

I didn't flinch. Still lying there, panting, on the bench, I looked straight up at him. 'I want in,' I said.

He blinked. He straightened. He looked down at me, surprised.

I sat up, swinging my feet to the ground. 'You said you could use me, right?'

He took a long, slow look around the yard to make sure no one was listening. Then he murmured softly, 'That's right. *If* you got what it takes.'

I stood. Instinctively, the other swastika boys circled around me, ready to attack if Blade gave the word.

'I've got what it takes,' I said. 'I want in. What do you say?'

Blade studied me a long minute. I'll tell you something: I'd already seen some truly evil humanoids in my life. Prince. Waylon. Orton. Not just guys who'd lost their way, you know, who'd made mistakes and done something wrong. I'm talking about the real evil-doing deal, the ones who knew they had a choice and chose to do damage to the rest of the world, who chose to cause suffering and wreak havoc. It's a special breed of truly wicked individual and I'd learned to know them when I saw them. And I knew Blade. Blade was right in there with the worst of them.

When he smiled, I felt a finger of ice draw itself slowly up my spine.

'Here's the deal,' he said in that grating purr. 'There's a reason we came to you, a reason we want you in.'

I nodded. 'I figured it wasn't my good looks. What is it?'

Blade looked around again, and all the other thugs looked around too. There was no one near us, no one who could hear.

Blade's low, rumbling growl went on. 'What I say next – there's no going back, you feel me? Once I let you in, you're in. You can't unknow what you know.'

I took a deep breath. If I could've thought of any other way to get out of here, to have some chance, some shot of finding out what the Great Death was, where it was going to take place, of stopping Prince before he could carry out his plan, believe me, I would've done it. But this was all I had.

I nodded. 'Keep talking.'

'Understand me, kid,' Blade went on. 'You play me for a fool, you play a double game with me, and you will die. Not maybe. Not probably. You will. No matter what happens to me. I got friends all over, friends everywhere. Once I tell you what we're planning, we are blood brothers, my young disciple, and, if you betray me, the gates of hell themselves will not keep me from having my revenge.'

All the time he was spouting this stuff, his eyes were glazed and dreamy. It was as if he was imagining his revenge as he spoke about it, imagining how sweet it would be. An evil dude, I'm telling you.

For my part, I knew I had to show Blade I wasn't intimidated. I was *way*, *way* intimidated, believe me. I'd've been crazy *not* to be intimidated. The guy was a stone-cold killer. But all the same, I knew I had to show him I was cool.

So I put on my hardest voice. I said, 'Yeah, yeah, yeah, Blade, I get it already. You're a tough guy and, if I mess with you, I'm a dead man. So you gonna tell me what I have to do or not?'

It sounded almost convincing – sort of. At least it made Blade smile: a big toothy grin. He looked around at his swastika pals. They toothy-grinned right back at him as if to give me their seal of approval. And it's funny – if by 'funny' you mean kind of miserable and strange – I have been tortured by terrorists; I've been shot at by the police; I've been taken away from my home, my family, my girl, just about everything I loved. But I don't think I ever felt quite so desperately far away from everything good and bright in the world as I felt just at that moment, surrounded by the smiling approval of this gang of racist madmen.

'OK,' said Blade. 'Listen up. About two miles from here, as the crow flies, there's a mall – or part of a mall – a mall they were building. You know, it was supposed to be for the town, Abingdon, where the guards and their families live and so on. Only times got tough, right? The builders ran out of money. The thing was never finished. It's just sitting out there off the main highway, all empty and abandoned – except not.'

I narrowed my eyes. I didn't get it. 'Not . . . ?' I said.

'Not really abandoned. Some of our friends have been working out there. Digging, if you see what I mean.'

I started to see, but I shook my head anyway to make sure he'd explain it all.

'See, the mall has a complete sewage system,' said Blade. 'And that system links up to the sewage system of the town. And that town system links up to a treatment plant. And that treatment plant also serves this prison.'

My lips parted. 'You mean, there's, like, a link between the

96

prison sewers and the sewers that go out to this abandoned mall?'

'That is what I mean. That's exactly what I mean.' Blade's dreaming eyes shifted back and forth as he went on. 'Our friends have been working round the clock to link the systems underground. Then it's an easy tunnel from the sewers right up into this yard right here.'

'The yard? What good does that do?' I said. 'We're surrounded by guns. The minute they break through the ground, the guards'll open fire.'

Blade grinned his toothy grin again and his pals grinned their toothy grins. Blade shook his head. 'As it happens, there's exactly one place in this entire prison where a tunnel could break through *without* being noticed by anyone.'

I thought about it for a minute, but I still didn't get it.

'The Outbuilding,' said Blade.

As he said the word, my eyes darted to the cinder-block structure sitting squat in the corner of the yard. A cold wind blew over me. It almost felt like some kind of warning, some kind of omen. It made me shiver, standing there, surrounded by those grinning and evil men.

'The Outbuilding,' I echoed softly.

'It's the Yard King's castle, no? He's in there alone most of the time. He likes it that way. No one sees what he does, no one hears what he says, no one knows what he's up to. If our friends can tunnel up into the Outbuilding, it's more than likely there'll be nobody there but Dunbar.'

I shrugged. 'So what? Dunbar doesn't need any help to set

off an alarm. All he has to do is shout . . .'

'But he's not gonna shout,' purred Blade. 'He's not gonna do anything.'

'Oh yeah? Why not?'

Once again, the wind rose. Once again, Blade smiled around at his friends and they smiled back.

'The thing about the Yard King,' Blade said, 'is that he holds a grudge.'

I gave a snorting, mirthless laugh. 'Yeah, I noticed that.'

'I'll bet you have. See, once he takes a dislike to you, nothing on this earth will keep you safe until he feels sure he's broken you or killed you. Until he knows you live in fear of him, until he sees you cringe and grovel every time he walks by, he will not let you be. That's how he is when he gets his grudge on against someone.'

'I know, I know.'

'You do know. Because right now, my young disciple, Yard King Dunbar has his grudge on against you.'

I nodded. 'He does. That's the truth. He's promised he'll get me back in that Outbuilding the first chance he gets.'

'Well, we're going to give him that chance,' Blade murmured. 'December 30th. Five days after Christmas.'

'The thirtieth . . . You said "right after." '

'That is right after. That's when the tunnel will be finished. That's the earliest we can go.'

I took a breath. December 30th. One day before New Year's Eve. How would I ever find Prince in time? How would I ever stop him?

Blade went on, 'Yard time the thirtieth, you are going to start some trouble in the yard. You are going to get into a fight with me, in fact. It is a sure thing what will follow that.'

I nodded. 'Dunbar'll have his goons drag me into the Outbuilding so he can beat the daylights out of me.'

Blade gave a laugh and the cold wind blew and, to tell you the truth, I wasn't sure which chilled me more, his laughter or the wind. 'That's right. That's exactly what he'll do. And as we learned in our last journey to the Outbuilding, when he takes you inside, the other guards disappear.'

'That's right. He doesn't want any witnesses.'

'And because he doesn't want any witnesses, you will be in there all alone with Yard King Dunbar at the very moment when our friends are ready to break through into the Outbuilding and give us a passage out of here.'

I looked into Blade's dreamy eyes to see if I could find any humanity in there. I shouldn't have wasted my time. I said, 'That's your master plan? What do you think? You think Dunbar won't set off the alarm because he'll be too busy beating me to a pulp?'

Blade gave that chilling laugh again. 'Oh, no, no, no, my young disciple. No, no, no. My master plan is to supply you with a shiv – a knife.' His toothy grin flashed and the toothy grins of the men around him flashed. Blade laid his hand on my shoulder.

'Dunbar is not going to set off the alarm,' he said, 'because you're going to kill him.'

PART II

Chapter Thirteen

Mike

On Christmas Eve, Sensei Mike came. I was counting on that. It was the best hope I had.

I was sitting on my stool in the visiting room. There was a prisoner on either side of me and a guard walking back and forth behind. I was looking out through my pane of glass, when Mike came down the hall. Just the sight of him seemed to put strength into me. For one second I found myself thinking, *This is going to work. This is going to be all right.*

Mike was wearing jeans and a kind of flowery shirt and a sports jacket. He never looked right to me out of his karate *gi*. He was a tall man, lean but with broad shoulders. He had a lot of black hair, which he was very proud of, and a thick black moustache behind which his mouth always seemed to be sort of bent in a mocking smile. There was always a smile in his eyes too – even now. Mike had seen some pretty awful things in the wars in the Middle East, I guess. He'd learned there was not too much stuff in life that needed to be taken seriously. Just the right stuff. Just enough.

Mike had taught me karate in his studio at the mall in my hometown, Spring Hill. But that's not all he'd taught me. In fact, it doesn't even begin to tell the story. Mike had taught me a whole way of thinking – a way of being, really. I was one kind of person when I started to study the martial arts as a little kid, and I was another kind of person when I finally got my black belt. A lot of the difference was because of Mike.

It wasn't just that I could fight now and protect myself – although, man, that sure had come in handy, hadn't it? But it was more the way Mike taught me to think. It was sort of like Mike told me the stuff in words and lessons that my father just showed me by the way he was. Mike taught me that, whatever the situation, whether I was outnumbered, out-smarted, or even beaten and at the end of my rope, I could always ask myself a simple question: how can I come out of this stronger? Better? Mike didn't talk about God or religion a lot. I saw him sometimes in his office paging through the cool camo-covered Bible they gave him in the Army, but he rarely talked about it. He just talked about karate. He talked about how, in karate, whether you did well or badly, whether you won or lost, whether you got good breaks or suffered bad luck, there was always a path forward – forward and upward: a path to a better, stronger life. He taught me that, if you look for that path hard enough, you will always find it. And when you find it, he said, even if you lose the fight, even if you lose everything, you can never lose, not really.

He taught me all that through the competitions I entered and in the back-breaking practices and tests I had to go through to earn my belts. And just knowing that, just knowing that there was always a path, made me different inside. I guess you could say it taught me how to be a man. I was grateful to Mike for that.

My point is, there was no one on the planet I trusted more. When Sensei Mike came down the hallway and sat on the stool across from mine and looked in through the window and picked up the phone, I felt better right away, that's all.

I picked up my phone and nodded at him. For a second or two, neither of us said anything.

Then Mike said, 'Well, chucklehead, here's another fine mess you've gotten yourself into. I can't leave you alone for ten minutes.'

I laughed. It felt like the first time I'd laughed in about a century. Hearing his voice just seemed to put steel in my backbone.

'So how's the worst prison in the country treating you?' he asked. He kept his eyes on mine and I knew he could already see the answer.

So I just said, 'Hey, no sweat. It's just like high school – only with murderers.'

His mouth curled under his moustache. 'You could almost consider that an improvement.'

'Right.'

We were silent again. There were a million things I wanted to say to him. I wanted to tell him the truth about this awful place. I wanted to tell him every evil thing I'd seen here. I wanted him to help me make sense of it and explain to me how you could do right in a place that was so wrong. But there wasn't time for anything like that. I had to talk fast – and I had to make sure no one around me heard. If what I was about to say got back to Blade and his friends, I'd be dead within the hour.

'Mike, listen, there's not a lot of time,' I said. 'I have to talk fast and you have to listen really well.'

Mike's smile disappeared. His face went very still very fast. 'Go,' he said.

'I don't know how much you know about why I'm here . . .'

He nodded once. 'All of it.'

Startled, I blinked and stared. 'How . . . ?'

'You remember the night you came to the dojo? The night you and I fought it out?'

'It wasn't much of a fight,' I said. 'As I recall, you kicked me around the room like a soccer ball.'

'And you told me you'd lost a year of memory. That you went to bed one night and woke up captured by terrorists, wanted by the police . . . I couldn't make any sense out of it at first, but when your friend, Mr Sherman, turned up dead . . .'

'Yeah, my friend,' I said sarcastically.

'I started to put things together. I've still got a lot of friends in the military, a lot of contacts in intelligence, special forces, all the secret places. I started asking around. I didn't get the whole story, but I got enough of it to get to Rose.'

My jaw literally dropped. My mouth hung open as I stared at him.

'Close your mouth, chucklehead. You look like an idiot,' he said.

My teeth clopped together. 'You talked to Rose?' I said. 'How did you know he was part of it?'

Mike shrugged. 'I just figured it out, you know. The way you escaped from his custody, the fact that he kept showing up out of his jurisdiction to hunt you down, taking charge of other police departments and stuff like that. That's not the way things work. Also, the fact that you were supposed to be this mad killer, but he somehow managed to hunt you down without you getting hurt. Like I said, I just figured it out.'

'Wow. That's amazing. I mean, *I* never even figured it out.'

'Well, you're a chucklehead, that's why.'

'Oh yeah. I forgot.'

'Anyway,' Mike went on. 'I thought maybe if I went to Rose and played the whole military card, showed him my medals, bled on his floor, whatever, I could get him to let me in on what was happening.'

'And did he?'

'Nah, you kidding? Guy stonewalled me into the ground. It was like talking to Mount Rushmore. But . . .' He wagged his big head of black hair back and forth. 'Let's just say there was a lot of information in some of those silences of his.'

The wave of surprise started to draw back inside me. I took stock of what he was telling me. Mike had a pretty good idea of what it was all about. And he knew Detective Rose was in on it. 'That's great,' I said, excited. 'That's great. Is there any way you could get in touch with him? With Rose, I mean?'

Mike stroked his moustache as he thought about it. 'Maybe. It wouldn't be easy. He told me he's gonna go invisible, but, like I say, I still got a lot of contacts in secret places. I might be able to get word to him somehow.'

My heart started pounding harder. A chance – a hope. I couldn't ask for more than that. I leaned in close to the glass, dropping my voice. I knew the prison authorities could listen in if they wanted. But as long as I didn't talk about Blade's escape plans, I didn't see where it made much difference. I'd already gone to the Warden, after all, so it was no secret I was worried about the Homelanders.

'All right,' I said. 'Here's the deal. Most of the Homelanders have been rounded up now, but not all of them. The leader, Prince, is still on the loose.'

Now it was Mike's turn to look surprised. 'Really? Rose gave me the impression it was all over . . .'

'I know. That's what the government thinks and what they want everyone to think. They figure Prince has left the country so there's no reason to start a panic. But they're wrong. He's still here.'

'How do you know?'

'I just do. Prince swore he wouldn't leave, wouldn't give up until he'd carried out a plan called the Great Death . . .'

'The Great Death, huh? I'm guessing that's not good.'

'That's my guess, too. It involves something called a CO

device that they're acquiring from the Russians. Any idea what that is?'

'No. But it must be a weapon of some kind.'

'Right,' I said. 'And whatever it is, they're going to set it off on the devil's New Year's Eve.'

'And the devil . . . ?'

'Is us, America, right?'

Mike sighed. 'Of course. Who else? OK. Where is this supposed to happen?' Mike was leaning into the glass on his side, too, now. His eyes were flat and serious. He knew there was no time to waste.

'I don't know,' I told him. 'I don't know if I ever knew. If I did, I don't remember. Right now, that's all I got.'

'OK.'

'You have to get the word out to Rose. You have to. If not to Rose, then to some of your other friends.'

'Don't worry. It's as good as done.'

I leaned in even closer. Our faces were inches apart now, with the glass between us. 'And Mike,' I said. 'You gotta get the word to Samuel.'

I saw his black eyebrows draw down. 'Samuel?'

'He's coming to town after Christmas. He'll be the first at number 1912 on the 30th December. Samuel, I mean.'

The next moment seemed to last forever. I didn't really think there was much of a chance that Mike would understand me then and there. Like I said, he did read that camo-covered Bible but I doubted he knew it chapter and verse. I was never much good at memorizing stuff myself. I had my copy in my cell, so I'd looked it up before coming. I just hoped Mike would figure out what I was trying to say and look it up himself when he got home.

'Samuel, the first at number 1912,' I heard him repeat softly. I saw his eyes move away from me and shift up to the right as if he were looking for something inside his own head. And then – yes! – I could see it on his face. He found it:

First Samuel 19.12: *So Michal let David down through a window, and he fled and escaped.*

Mike's lips parted. He understood. He stared at me, dumbfounded.

'December 30th,' I said again. 'He'll be there with all his friends.'

Mike's face changed as I watched through the window. For a minute, I seriously thought he was going to come crashing through that Plexiglas and grab me by the shirt. His voice became a harsh whisper. 'Are you out of your mind? I said I'd get the word out and I will.'

'There's no time, Mike. You're gonna need whatever information is in my head. It might be our only chance.'

'Forget it,' Mike said, his eyes burning into me. 'We'll handle it from here.'

'You're going to need friends, too. Rose is going to need them. He's on the outs with his bosses. He's an embarrassment to them and they don't believe him. Even if he finds the answers he needs, he may be on his own.'

'No,' Mike told me, speaking full force. 'It's nuts. Nuts. Do – not – do – it. You read me?'

'Mike—'

'Do you read me, chucklehead?'

I sat back. What could I say? Mike was smart. Not just smart. He was wise. He was a soldier, a hero, and if he said he was going to get to Rose, he would get to him, if anyone could.

But the truth is, I was breaking out of here, anyway. I didn't know what the Great Death meant – not exactly – but I knew Prince would not be satisfied with anything less than massive murder and destruction. I could not sit inside my cell and just hope he was stopped. If I could help, I had to try.

'Do you read me?' Mike said once again.

'*Time's up!*'

I started as the guard made the announcement over the loudspeaker. Mike kept leaning in toward me, waiting for my answer. But now the two guards who stood on watch behind the visitors came forward off the wall.

'Wrap it up,' one of them said.

Mike stared in at me through the glass. 'I will get the word out,' he told me. 'There is no need to do anything stupid.'

'Mike,' I said. 'If anything happens, if New Year's Eve comes and Prince isn't stopped and I thought I could've done something . . .'

'No,' he said again.

'Listen to me . . .'

A hand came down on my shoulder. It was the guard behind me. 'Say "Merry Christmas," kid, and wrap it up,' he said. 'You're done.'

'Merry Christmas, Mike,' I said. Slowly, my hand lifted to set the telephone back in its cradle. Mike was still talking through his handset. I could see him shaking his head. I could see his lips forming the word, 'No,' over and over again.

The guard came up behind him and said something I couldn't hear. Mike hung up the phone – hard. He stood up. We stared at each other through the glass.

Mike shook his head one more time. No.

Then the guard led me away.

Chapter Fourteen

Merry Christmas

I got the knife on Christmas Day – the shiv I was supposed to kill Dunbar with. Blade slipped it into my hand during the service in the chapel.

The chapel was just another faceless, windowless cinder-block room in the prison. The cinder blocks were painted yellow here instead of green. And, during Christian services, there was a cross hung on the wall. Today, for Christmas, there was also a wreath and a small wooden crèche set up on the table that the Chaplain used for his lectern. For Abingdon, the place was almost cheery.

The Chaplain was named Chaplain Adams. He was an old black guy – I don't know how old, but old. He had long, sad features that looked like he was mourning for the world. I'd only had a chance to talk to him once, but I got the impression he was the only semi-decent human being in the whole prison. Maybe that's why he always looked so sad.

He had his big leather Bible open on the table next to the crèche. He was reading the Christmas passages in Luke. His voice was as sad as his face. Even the joyful words of the scripture sounded mournful when he said them:

'And the Angel said to them, "Fear not: For behold, I bring you good tidings of great joy, which shall be to all people . . ." '

Hard to make that sound mournful but somehow Chaplain Adams managed to do it.

There were a lot of folding chairs packed into the room. They were full – a prisoner in each – guys of every color who'd committed all kinds of crimes – praying. Most of them sincere, I'd guess. Looking for a way out of a bad past, and a path to a better life.

I know I was sincere. I was sitting in a chair about halfway to the back of the room, off to the right of center. I had my head bowed, my eyes closed. And I was praying just about as hard as I could. I was praying for help, praying that Mike would get word to Rose, and that Rose would get word to his bosses in Washington, and that his bosses in Washington would turn out full force to find Prince – and that everything would be taken care of by somebody else so that I wouldn't have to break out of here with a bunch of Nazi maniacs.

Your will be done, I added at the end of my prayer – but I've got to admit, I didn't really mean it. I really wanted *my* will to be done: namely, I wanted God to get me out of this mess, and fast!

Anyway, I was hard at it, my head bowed, my eyes closed, so I didn't really notice when the prisoner next to me got up and moved away. The first I noticed was when I felt the smooth plastic tube slip into my hand.

My head came up fast, my eyes opened fast. There was Blade, suddenly sitting next to me. His dreamy, murderous eyes were fixed on mine.

I looked down and saw what he had given me. A home-made knife. I don't know what it had been originally. Part of a bed or a chair, maybe. I don't know. It was a tubular piece of thick plastic with string wound tight around one end to make a handle grip. The other end was sharpened to a long, deadly point.

When I looked up at Blade again, he smiled his toothy smile. He slowly pressed his index finger under his chin to show me how to drive the knife into Dunbar's throat. But, of course, I had already pretty much figured that's what he wanted me to do.

Then, with a quick glance around to make sure no one was watching us, Blade reached over and gently pushed the shiv up into my sleeve.

'Just call me Santa Claus,' he whispered.

Then he bowed his head and closed his eyes and pretended that he was praying, too. And I bowed my head and closed my eyes – only I wasn't pretending.

' "And the shepherds returned," ' read Chaplain Adams mournfully, ' "glorifying and praising God for all the things that they had heard and seen, as it was told to them." '

Chapter Fifteen

Dunbar Again

'Yard time!'

There was a flurry of snow falling as I stepped out into the yard. The sky was dark gray again and hung low over the heads of the gray prisoners moving over the grass and asphalt. The watchtowers seemed almost black against the sky. The riflemen inside were just slowly pacing silhouettes.

I felt the plastic knife against the flesh of my wrist. It was pushed up my sleeve and secured there tightly by a couple of loops of cloth I'd attached the night before.

As I moved through the cold air to the weight area where Blade and his fellow thugs were working out, I glanced over in the direction of the Outbuilding. There was Dunbar, surrounded by his guards, watching me pass.

I reached Blade. Blade smiled. His eyes were far away. He seemed lost in his dreams, whatever sick and murderous dreams they were.

'All right,' I said. 'When do you want to—?'

Blade punched me.

It was a short, sharp shot that took me totally by surprise. It wasn't faked. It wasn't pulled. It connected with my jaw full strength.

Before I even felt the pain of it, I was sprawled on my back with dust flying up around me. Sparks seemed to be dancing in front of my eyes.

Through the dust and the sparks, I saw Blade coming at me.

Before I could clear my head, he kicked me in the ribs – hard. There was nothing fake about that either. Blade was having too much fun to hold back. He cocked his foot to kick again.

I swiveled on my backside, fast, swung my legs around and kicked his standing leg out from under him.

Blade went down. I leapt on top of him, driving my fist hard into his face as I did. Instantly, the other cons were circling us, cheering. Blade and I rolled over and over in the dust, clawing at one another's eyes, pounding at one another's ribs. He wasn't pretending, so I didn't pretend either: I had to defend myself or, escape plan or not, I think he would've just knocked me flat out for the fun of it. Fortunately, locked together like that, neither of us could put much force into our blows. There was a lot of action, but not much damage being done.

What did hurt was the walkie-talkie the guard hit me with.

He used the heavy butt of the thing and drove it down into the back of my head as Blade and I rolled over in the dirt.

Instantly, the pain shot through my entire body. My thoughts went foggy. My limbs went weak.

Guards grabbed me by the arms. They hauled Blade off me. Blade sent a final kick into my ribs for good measure as they dragged me away.

Now there were three guards holding me, one guard gripping either arm and a third one grabbing me by the collar. They frogmarched me across the yard, my chin on my chest, my head lolling back and forth. As my mind began to clear, I lifted my eyes and saw the Outbuilding coming toward me, getting larger and larger. Larger and larger too was the grinning, eager fist-face of Dunbar. His eyes were alight with the anticipation of beating up on me again. I knew, if he had his way, the beating was going to be much, much worse this time.

The guards manhandled me into the Outbuilding, tossing me through the door so that I stumbled across the room. I hit the far wall and sank to my knees.

I was now in a dark bunker of a place, an open space with its gray cinder-block walls lit by dangling bulbs. There was a small office in one corner, created with metal dividers. There were crates of I-don't-know-what stacked here and there. This was where the Yard King did whatever it was he did when no one was looking.

The guards followed me to where I lay on the hard-packed dirt floor. One of them kicked me in the stomach so that I curled up, clutching myself. Another kicked me in the back so that I straightened, letting out a cry of pain. My cry disappeared underneath a hollow roaring sound that seemed to fill every corner of the Outbuilding. That was the heating system blowing warm air through the place.

Then, smirking, the guards withdrew, leaving the Outbuilding and closing the door behind them.

Now I was alone with Dunbar.

When I was able to look, I saw the Yard King standing over me. Slowly, painfully, I raised my eyes from his shoe tips and blinked up at him. For a long moment, he was just a foggy figure seen dimly through a haze of pain. Bit by bit, the haze passed and he came into focus. It wasn't a pleasant sight.

The thick, squat man stood with his legs akimbo. His knuckly face looked down at me. Nastiness seemed to come off him in waves. His cheeks were flushed with it and his eyes almost seemed to glow. When he spoke, it was with the voice of a volcano: it sounded as if it were coming from some hot, bubbling place deep down inside him. It was as if he could hardly contain the thrill he felt at the idea of pounding me half to death.

'What did you think, garbage boy?' he said. The sound of that voice burned right through me. 'When you were talking tough in the infirmary. Huh? What did you think?' He nudged me with the tip of his shoe. 'I'm asking you a question.'

I groaned in answer. It was all I could manage.

'When you put your hands on me like I was just one of your fellow garbage cons,' Dunbar went on, 'what exactly were you thinking? Really – I'm curious to know.' He nudged me again. 'Did you think you'd never be back here? Did you think I'd never get another chance at you?' He let out a brief laugh. He shook his head. 'You cons are so dumb. Don't you understand? In here, behind these walls, time is always on my side. Always. Eventually, I always get my chance.'

I flinched as he crouched down over me. He grinned at that. He liked to see my fear. He chuckled.

Carefully I slipped the knife out of my sleeve into my palm. I wrapped my fingers around the rope-grip handle.

'Oh, you con, you garbage,' Dunbar said, shaking his head again. 'Let me tell you something: this is gonna hurt you way, way more than it hurts me.' He reached down to grab me.

And then I was on him.

I don't think I'd ever moved so fast in my life. I wasn't sure what was going to happen next – when the escape would begin or how or when – but I knew it was going to be soon, any minute, and there was no time to lose.

Before Dunbar could react, before he could even get that sadistic grin off his face, I sprang off the floor and grabbed him by the hair. At the same time, I threw a body block into him. Crouched down the way he was, he was completely off balance. I drove him to the floor and got on top of him, my knees pinning his arms, my knife-blade set against the soft flesh under his chin.

I pressed my face close to his. I spoke in a low whisper, the words tumbling out quickly.

'Listen to me, Dunbar. Listen to me good. Any second now, some of Blade's thug pals are gonna come through that wall. You read me, chucklehead?'

Dunbar couldn't believe what was happening. He couldn't understand what I was saying. 'What?'

I banged his head against the floor. 'Listen! I'm supposed to kill you now, do you understand me?'

'I . . .'

I banged his head again. 'Do you?'

He nodded quickly. 'Yes! Yes! Don't kill me! Please!'

'It doesn't matter whether I do or not. If I don't kill you, you can bet Blade or one of his crazies will, OK?'

'Please,' he said again, terrified.

'You got one chance, one choice, which is to do what I tell you to do, you read me?'

'Yes, yes, anything, what?'

'Act dead. Play dead. Understand? Play dead or you will *be* dead. That's a guarantee.'

Before he could answer, I let him go. His head fell back against the floor. Before he could think, I took the knife away from his throat and held it to my arm. Taking a quick breath against the pain, I cut myself – a nice long slash.

Man, it hurt. It hurt like you wouldn't believe. A long second of pure, stinging pain. Then the thick blood began to flow. Dunbar tried to lift his head, but I jammed my arm under his throat, knocking him back, making him gag. I rubbed the arm back and forth against him so that my blood was smeared all over him. It wasn't going to look convincing, but I hoped it would do the trick in the rush and confusion that was sure to come.

I jumped off the Yard King. It wasn't easy to move, let me

tell you. I had to ignore the pain all over my body from all the punishment I'd taken. But I did ignore it. What had to be done had to be done.

I grabbed Dunbar by the shirtfront and hauled him up to his knees. I dragged him to a dark corner of the Outbuilding as he struggled to get his feet under him. All the while I was dragging him, I was talking to him under my breath.

'There's a mall near here,' I told him. 'An unfinished mall about two miles away. You know it?'

'Yeah. Yeah,' Dunbar said weakly.

'That's where Blade and his boys are headed. Tell the cops. You got it? Tell the cops to cut them off. Stop them. Don't let these clowns escape. They're killers, every one of them.'

I threw him against the wall. He sat down hard, his back pressed to the cinder blocks.

'Lie down and play dead, Dunbar,' I said. 'They'll be here any second and, if you don't look dead, you will be.'

I heard a noise behind me. I turned – but there was no one else in the Outbuilding. Not yet, anyway.

Suddenly, while I was turned like that, Dunbar grabbed my arm.

I spun around on him, drawing back the knife to threaten him.

But he wasn't on the attack. He was too stunned and scared for that. He was just gaping up at me, his eyes wide, his mouth open.

'Why . . . ?' he whispered.

'What?'

'Why didn't you do it?'

I shook my head. I didn't understand him.

'You were supposed to kill me,' said Dunbar. 'Why didn't you?'

For another second, I still couldn't figure out what he was saying. But then I got it: he really didn't know. He really didn't understand.

'I beat you,' he said. 'I'd've beat you again, worse this time, much worse. I might have killed you and you know it. Now you had your big chance. Why didn't you kill me?'

Angrily, I yanked my arm free of his grasp. He fell back against the wall.

'I haven't got time to explain it to you, Dunbar,' I said. 'Try to figure it out for yourself.'

The Yard King seemed about to speak again – but then he tensed, afraid. All at once, he slumped over and lay on the floor, his eyes shut, his mouth open. At first, I thought he'd fainted. But then I realized he was pretending to be dead.

That's when I looked over my shoulder and saw the hole in the dirt floor.

Blade's people had arrived.

Chapter Sixteen

Breakout

The entrance to the tunnel seemed to have appeared silently. At first, it was just a small break in the base of the cinder blocks. I could see the edge of a pickaxe working at it, prying off chunks of dirt, making the hole larger. How they had broken through so quietly, I don't know, but I guess at least some of the noise had been covered up by the roar of the heating system. In any case, now I could see a pair of bright eyes peering up at me from the darkness beneath.

What happened next happened quickly but in the same weird dream-like quiet. With any noise covered by the blasting air, it seemed like a silent movie. Blade and three of his fellow muscle-men suddenly stepped through the Outbuilding door.

I was stunned by how easy it was. 'Where are the guards outside?'

'Some of our boys have them distracted,' Blade said. 'Come on.'

Then I was moving with them, surrounded by them. We

were at the wall, at the break in the floor. Quickly, one by one, we were kneeling down. I watched two men wriggle through the break and disappear into the darkness.

I saw Blade cast a look across the long room at Dunbar. I followed his gaze. The Yard King was lying sprawled in the shadows at the far end of the room. You could just make out the dark stain of blood – my blood – on his throat and on the front of his shirt. I had been right. Moving as quickly as we were, he looked plenty dead enough to pass.

Blade nodded at me. 'Good work,' he said. 'I didn't think you had it in you.'

Then he went down to the ground and lowered himself through the hole.

I watched the top of his head sink down into nothingness. Then I lowered myself after him.

The moment I went over the side, I felt the ground open beneath my feet. My fingers touched a rope. I took hold of it. Wrapping my feet around it, I started sliding down. Blade was directly under my feet. Another man – the last man – was sliding down directly above my head.

Then we were on the ground somewhere below the earth. We were moving quickly in a tightly packed group through the darkness. There were flashlight beams lancing the black air, but they didn't illuminate much: a wall, the shoulder of a gray uniform, a face, taut and eager, moving forward. All of us were moving fast.

There were noises: rapid breaths, grunts of effort, curses, quick, padding footsteps. Now and then, a voice:

'This way.'

'Quick.'

'Out of my way.'

'Come on.'

I kept stumbling forward through the blackness.

After a while, I had the sense I was descending. It was hard to tell in the dark. I heard a splash, up ahead. Then the smell – what a stink! – washed up over me. Seconds later, I splashed into it too. The smell rose around me like smoke, wrapped itself around me, choking me, like smoky fingers on my throat.

I understood we were moving through the sewers now.

After that, there were turns and drops and climbs. Dancing flashlight beams. Glimpses of faces. A confusion of motion. There were moments when we were on some dry surface and moments when we were plunged thigh-deep in awful stinking mess. Soon, it all seemed to run together, a long, dark nightmare of panting motion through a nauseating stench. On and on we went, traveling through the connecting tunnels and tubes.

I don't know how long we ran. Sometimes we slowed to a kind of jog, but there was no stopping. I was afraid my strength would give out, but no. I could practically feel the adrenaline pumping through me, the energy surging in my limbs, unbelievably steady and unstoppable. My whole inner world was filled with the rhythm of my heart hammering and my lungs working. The pain – the pain I knew was pulsing in every part of me – the pain I knew was still there, always there

– seemed somehow far away for the moment, buried beneath the electric surface of that pumped-up adrenaline high. The punches from Blade, the beating from the guards, the cut I'd dug into my own flesh with the knife: yeah, they throbbed and ached and stung as I pushed myself to keep moving, but the ache seemed almost to belong to someone else, not me.

I ran and ran, breathless. I tried to get my brain working as we went down another corridor of stink and mess. One thing was on my mind and one thing only: we were rushing into a trap.

I had tipped Dunbar off. I had told him we were heading for the mall. I didn't know how long it would take him to sound the alarm or how fast the police would respond or how far they had to travel. But if the cops weren't waiting for us at the mall when we got there, they would get there soon enough. That would make it tough for me to get away. I would have to make my escape not just from Blade but from the cops as well. I wished I hadn't had to do it, to tell Dunbar the plan. But I couldn't just let this killer, Blade, and his pals escape. I had to make sure they were captured again. I just didn't see any other choice.

All this raced through my mind as I raced through the darkness. Stumbling along in the stench and wet. Crushed in with these thugs as they rushed desperately toward what they thought was freedom – a freedom I knew they would never have.

At last, panting, flagging, stumbling, we came around a bend in the dark corridor and I heard several voices at once.

'There.'

'Oh, man!'

'I see it! I see it!'

I saw it, too: light. A dim gray glow that seemed to pour down into the darkness like water. It was the way out, the way back to the upper world.

I could feel the others around me tense with hope and expectation. I could hear the beat of their breathing change. As the flashlight beams criss-crossed this way and that around us, I could see their faces, their bright, desperate faces, suddenly full of hope, their gazes yearning for that light up ahead, yearning for freedom.

More whispers:

'Oh yeah, yeah, yeah.'

'Baby, there we go.'

'We are going home.'

We all want the same thing, I guess. Killers or no, good or bad. We all want to be free. We all want to go home.

I looked ahead, down the tunnel, at the cascade of faint gray light growing brighter as we grew near. I was thinking, *What now? What do I do when the police surround us? How do I break away?*

I didn't know the answer and not knowing made me afraid. What if I made a run for it and the cops opened fire and shot me down? What if the cops showed up and Blade guessed I had tipped them off and *he* killed me?

What if – here was the really bad one – what if I tried to run and got captured again? My lawyer's appeal would be ruined. Even with all the help Rose had given me, no one would believe I was innocent now.

That thought made my inner world darken even as we moved to the light ahead. It was one thing to think about getting shot to death, it was something else – something much worse – to think about getting stuck in Abingdon for the rest of my life.

As we covered the last few yards to that gray glow, I tried to remind myself why I had done this: the Great Death. I had to stop it. I had to try, no matter what. No matter what.

I fought off my fears and pushed on.

The pavement beneath us was climbing now. Barely running, barely jogging, we just stumbled upward, exhausted, step by wobbly step. As we came near the light, I could make out the faces and forms of the men with me. They were all so exhausted that even the cruelty seemed to be gone from their eyes. There was just the desperation and yearning – to be free, to go home.

Blade was the lead man. He took a last step into the falling light. He stopped. He looked up. Captured in the gray glow, his scarred face with its devilish, pointed beard seemed washed clean by light. He looked young and fresh and almost innocent – the meanness gone. I guess he'd really been that way once, when he was a kid maybe, before he did the things he'd done. For a second, in that light, you could see how he used to be.

'Let's go,' he whispered up into the glow.

The next moment, a rope dropped down. Blade grabbed it,

wrapped his legs around it and started climbing up into the light.

As soon as there was room beneath his feet, another muscleman grabbed hold and started climbing. I was third in line. I went up the rope quickly, following the soles of the feet above me.

As I reached the top, a hand grabbed my arm, helping me up. I crawled out through a jagged hole. The smell and filth and weariness still clung to me. Blinking and squinting, I looked around at a world that seemed to have been drained of all color, that seemed only black and white, like an old movie.

I was in an empty structure, a half-finished building. The walls, floor and ceiling were all white cement and plaster. At the windows – or the spaces where windows were supposed to be – empty rectangles with no glass in them – there was a weird gray-blackness that I couldn't identify for a second. Then I could: it was the sky. It was covered to the horizon with thick, big-bellied clouds. A thunderstorm was gathering – gathering fast. I could feel the cold wet wind blowing in on me through the window holes.

I saw now that I was in an unfinished building. There were two men in overalls who had been waiting for us here. There were two others who had come into the prison to get us. Then there was Blade and his three companions, the final two of them still coming up the ropes.

Moving to one of the windows, I looked out. It was a strange sight: a ghost mall. Empty white structures everywhere like some desert city dug up by archaeologists or something. Window holes and sidewalks, some of them completed, others full of gaps and broken bits, all of it making for a geometric pattern of white cubes with dark rectangles in them. The whiteness of the mall buildings was set against the growing darkness of the clouds around. The clouds seemed to go on and on forever over empty territory. Beyond the mall, as far as I could see, there was nothing but dead fields full of dirt and boulders and sudden slopes that fell away out of sight.

I peered out and scanned the area. I was trying to pick out my best escape route. Behind me, I heard the last of the thugs grunting and cursing, climbing up through the broken hole in the building's floor. I wondered, *Could I just throw myself out the broken window and run for it?*

A movement at the corner of my eye caught my attention. I turned to it. My breath stopped.

A long line of white cars was moving toward the mall under the black clouds.

The police. Moving without sirens or lights over the long road through the empty country.

Coming. Coming here. Coming for us.

If I was going to run for it, I had to start running now.

There was a deep throaty roll of thunder.

I glanced back at the others to see if anyone was watching me.

Someone was: Blade. Not just watching me. He was pointing a gun at my head.

Chapter Seventeen

Thunderstorm

The thunder rolled again. Lightning flashed – sheet lightning that turned all the dark windows silver-white.

Blade held his arm stretched out straight in front of him, the barrel of the 9mm automatic in his hand leveled at the spot right between my eyes. That barrel and its cold, black bore were less than a yard away from me.

Blade didn't know the police were coming yet. He didn't know he had only seconds of freedom left. He took his time. He smiled his faraway smile, full of his bizarre, dreamy joy at dealing death.

'Thanks for the help, punk,' he said.

And he pulled the trigger.

By then, I had already sent my kick flying up in his direction, my foot sweeping in a broad crescent from the floor to his hand. The side of my shoe connected with his wrist at the same moment the gun went off. I felt the cold kiss of death speed past my cheek as the bullet missed me by inches.

Then Blade's hand went wide and the gun flew from his fingers, twirling through the air, down toward the floor.

Before it even landed, I was at the open window. I grabbed hold of the sill and leapt through.

'Grab him!' Blade shouted – but whatever else he might've said was drowned out by another loud blast of thunder.

I landed upright on the pavement outside the building. At the same moment my feet touched the ground, the sky opened and the rain came. There was no build-up. No slow drizzle of warning. It came down in a sudden flood, as if a trapdoor had opened in the sky and the water was just dumped through it.

I ran. Away from the line of cop cars still racing toward us out of the wilderness. The second I started moving, I heard their sirens wind up behind me. They screamed into the sky – and then were drowned out by the next roll of thunder as the rain spilled down, drenching me.

I raced across the mall pavement, already kicking up puddles where the water had collected in the broken spaces. The silver splashes fanned into the dark air in front of me as I dashed through the open for the shelter of the abandoned white buildings across the way.

Another crack of thunder – and I saw a spark and a cloud of white plaster explode off the wall ahead of me. Silent gunfire – the sound of the shot drowned out by the storm.

I glanced back and saw Blade, the murder burning in his eyes, leveling the 9mm to take yet another crack at me.

But, at the same time, the sirens of the cop cars got louder as the army of police descended on the place. Behind Blade, I could see his panicked buddies rolling out the windows, scrambling toward a couple of pick-up trucks – the getaway vehicles they had parked around the side.

Blade's eyes shifted just slightly to see how much time he had left. His so-called friends weren't going to wait for him with the police so close – he knew that. He leveled the gun at me for one last shot.

But, before he could take it, I had faced front. I had reached the buildings on the other side of the mall lane. I pushed off my foot to dodge to the side. I slipped on the wet pavement, tumbling down on to my shoulder, rolling through the downpour until I could leap to my feet again.

This time, I heard the gun go off: a loud blast echoing through the storm. This time, the bullet was nowhere near me. My own dodge and fall had carried me out of Blade's line of fire. Another cloud of white dust exploded off one of the abandoned buildings, the powder rising into the dark rain. The sirens screamed and the thunder drowned them out and then the thunder fell away and the sirens screamed again.

As I regained my feet, I looked back once more. Blade was reluctantly turning away to join the others in their trucks. The engines started. The headlights split the darkness, lighting the downpour. With a screech of tires, the trucks pulled away from the curb, sending sheets of water into the air.

I was running again, meanwhile, in the opposite direction – across the large mall parking lot into the alleys; between the far buildings where it would be hard for the police cars to follow. Each time I broke out into the open, I dodged to the side and rushed toward another alley – down it – through. The rain was falling so hard now it nearly blinded me, but it didn't really matter. There was nowhere to go except out of the mall, out into the open country away from the roads. Anything that might make it difficult for the cop cars to follow me.

I ran through that empty, abandoned mall as fast as I'd ever run. Battered, beaten, exhausted from our long trek through the sewers, drenched now from the downpour: none of it mattered. I just ran.

As I reached the edge of the pavement, as I crossed the border into the surrounding wilderness, I glanced back one last time.

The escape was over – that fast; that completely. Through the curtains of rain, I could make out the shapes of Blade's two getaway trucks. They had come to a standstill, cut off and surrounded by the police cars. The cops were on the pavement, kneeling behind their cars, guns drawn and leveled. I could see their wavering silhouettes through the rain. The wavering silhouettes of the thugs were pouring out of the trucks with their hands up. There was no shooting. There was no point, nowhere for them to run. Our race through the sewer was all the freedom they were going to get.

I turned and pushed on, gasping, over the edge of the pavement. My feet sank into soggy earth as I scrambled through an empty field of mud and stone that went on as far as I could see – which wasn't far. The rain pretty much blinded me.

I plunged over the edge of a ridge before I even knew the ridge was there. The next second, I was lurching downhill, my legs barely under control as my long strides carried me over the steep slope. I descended into a small flat with low hills on every side of me. I had no idea which direction was which, or what was up ahead. I just ran on, climbing up a slope, half upright, half slipping and sliding, my fingers digging for purchase in the mud.

I came over the slope and stood still for a second, panting. Trying to get my bearings, trying to see where I should go. There was nothing around me but hills – hills of dirt – and rain turning the dirt to sludge. The great dark clouds churned above me. Thunder rolled. Lightning struck with a snake-like hiss – a jagged electric line this time. It reached all the way down from the sky to strike the earth maybe a mile or so up ahead of me. I held my breath at the awesome sight of it.

The rain plastered my hair to my scalp. The water poured into my eyes and into my open mouth as I stood panting for breath. I shivered from the cold.

Finally, I chose a direction. I started running again.

I had taken only a single step, when an engine roared and a pair of headlights came flying over the hill in front of me.

Chapter Eighteen

Run Down

It was a massive Jeep, jumping the ridge. The sight of it froze me in my tracks. Where had it come from? We were far from any road, far from anything. There was nothing out here but me and the mud – and those glaring headlights and those monster tires and that grinning grill.

The next instant, the Jeep smacked down, throwing up sheets of dirt and water. At the same time, I started running again, my feet nearly skidding out from under me as I changed direction and tried to get out of the Jeep's way.

The headlights bore down on me as I cut straight across them. The Jeep passed behind me so close, I felt the mud spatter over my back as I ran. I climbed desperately up the slope ahead of me as the Jeep, unable to stop, splashed up the slope to my left.

I heard its tires whining as they spun in the mud. I heard a voice begin to shout – or thought I did. But the next moment I could hear nothing but thunder.

As I reached the top of the ridge, I could feel the earth,

turned to gushing mud, sliding away under my feet. I threw myself forward and rolled. Gasping for breath, covered head to foot in filth, I climbed to my knees, peering around through the blinding rain.

There was nothing to see – nothing in any direction but empty territory and boiling black clouds and the streaking downpour.

As the thunder died, I heard the Jeep's tires spinning again. Then I heard them catch traction. I heard the engine's roar grow throaty and deep. A moment later, I heard that roar getting louder and louder. The Jeep had finally turned around and was heading back toward me again.

I ran. My speed was gone now. My energy had at last given out. My legs were weak and wobbly beneath me. My lungs were burning. My wet, muddy clothes were so heavy I felt like I was wearing a suit of lead, dragging it through the storm. Only my will was still strong. I was determined not to surrender, determined to make them run me down, make them overtake me. The idea of being taken back to that prison was a living nightmare.

I stumbled on, my arms wheeling, my hands grasping as if to find purchase in the driving rain. The lightning snapped and flashed across the black sky. The Jeep's engine strained as the car tried to make its way up the slope behind me.

I looked back over my shoulder just in time to see the dark rain go bright as those huge headlights crested the ridge. In the next second, the Jeep leapt into sight and plunged down into the mud, splattering dirt everywhere as it charged relentlessly after me.

I poured everything I had left into the next few seconds. But it was no good, no use. I was exhausted. I was done. The Jeep's horn screamed at my back like the cry of a hungry animal. The engine roared louder as the big machine overtook my failing footsteps.

The next time I looked, the headlights were enormous, filling my vision. The Jeep was right on top of me, seconds from plowing over me.

I leapt to the side and, as I did, I lost my footing and fell. I went down into the mud, clawing at it, rolling, trying to stand. I heard the Jeep's brakes shriek as its wheels locked. Scrabbling over the shifting, muddy ground, I saw the big vehicle go skidding past me through the mud, turning so that its headlights seemed to search for me in the dark. The rain was so heavy the headlights blurred. The Jeep was almost invisible though it was only a few yards away from me.

Now, unable to stand, I started crawling. It was the best I could do. I clawed my way across the earth, my face inches from the mud, my hands and knees and feet sinking deep into the mess of it.

The Jeep had stopped moving. Behind me, I heard its door open and shut. The thunder rolled and the lightning flashed. When the noise subsided, I heard the wet footsteps of my pursuer. I saw his tall figure moving toward me in the glow of the headlights. I didn't know whether he was coming to arrest or to kill me dead.

Finally, out of breath, out of strength, I collapsed into the mud. The footsteps came nearer and stopped. The Jeep's driver was standing over me.

I lay where I was, panting into the earth. I couldn't go any further. I just managed to roll on to my back and peer up through the rain at the figure above me.

'Come on, chucklehead, get in the stupid car,' he said.

It was Mike.

PART III

Chapter Nineteen

Flashes

Mike grabbed me under the arms and hauled me up. My legs felt like spaghetti, my lungs like fire. Mike half dragged me to the Jeep as I struggled to get my feet under me. When we reached the side of the vehicle, he pulled the door open and dropped me on to the passenger seat. He left me there to struggle the rest of the way in.

By the time I got the door shut, he was in the driver's seat beside me. He didn't say another word, just hit the gas. The tires spun and mud spat up around us. Then the rubber gripped the ground and the Jeep started moving through the rain.

I was curled up on my side, my cheek pressed into the seat back. My mouth hung open as I wheezed for air. The mud and rain were dripping off me. My head was spinning with exhaustion. I wasn't even sure this was really happening, that it was really real.

'Mike . . . ?' I tried to say through my gasps. My voice was barely audible over the engine noise, even to me.

'There's fresh clothes in the back,' Mike said, working the wheel, staring hard through the windshield. 'Get into them. There's some food back there, too.'

'Water . . .'

'Yeah, a couple of bottles.'

Desperate for a drink, I managed to find the strength to twist around and reach into the back seat. I found a water bottle and sucked hard on the nozzle, swallowing gulp after gulp. Then I fell back weakly against the seat back again.

'What're you . . . ?' It took me two tries to finish the sentence. 'What're you doing here, Mike? How did you . . . ?'

'Long story, chucklehead,' said Mike. 'And right now, I'm busy trying not to drive into a ditch or get caught by the police. Take a break, change, eat, get some rest. I'll get us out of here.'

So we were silent for a while. The Jeep bounced and skidded and juddered over the mud through the rain. The thunder crashed. The lightning split the sky. But it all seemed far away now, further and further away . . .

I wanted to change out of my wet, muddy clothes. I wanted to eat. But I couldn't move. I was just too tired. My eyes sank shut. I felt the world sinking away from me . . .

A flash. Not lightning this time. This time, it was inside my brain. A flash of light – and I was there again, in the past again. In the Homelanders' forest compound. Crouched in the night outside the lighted barracks, listening through the window to the voices of the people inside: Prince, Waylon, Sherman –

discussing their plans to assassinate the new head of Homeland Security. And then . . .

Even if I have to do it on my own, the Great Death will not be stopped. The basic elements are already in place. Come what may, it will ring in the devil's new year. I will make sure of it personally, if I have to.

'Not yet, chucklehead.'

My eyes snapped open at the rough bark of Mike's voice.

'What?' I murmured. 'Where am I?'

'You fall asleep in those clothes, you'll wake up with pneumonia. Plus, if a cop does stop us, he'll see your prison gear. You gotta change first. Then you can sleep.'

The past – that moment outside the barracks – was tantalizingly close. I could almost see it, almost remember what had happened next. The scene continued to flicker in my mind. Pieces of it appeared like images on a broken TV, then fizzled back into darkness . . .

Someone – the guard? – grabbed me by the shoulder . . .

But Mike was right. I was already shivering. My fingers felt stiff and my lips unsteady. The mud was crusting on me. I had to change.

I tried to remember that night in the Homelanders' compound as I forced my limbs to move, forced myself to lift up and half climb over, half slither between the front seats into the narrow seat in the back. My mouth hung open with exhaustion as I lifted up a gray sweat suit with an Army logo.

★

I turned in the dark, knowing they would kill me if they found me. It was the guard . . . He'd caught me . . . His bright eyes stared at me, full of rage . . .

Then the scene was gone again, like the name of a song you can't quite remember.

I twisted around in the small space, working out of my muddy clothes. It felt good to get the dry sweatsuit on me. Its fabric was warm from being inside the car. Then I found a heavy Yankees baseball jacket. I slipped into that, too.

The guard is about to shout. Prince will hear him. Waylon will hear him. They'll discover me. Kill me . . .

The Jeep bounced and bounded, nearly throwing me on to the floor. I braced myself in the tight space. When the ride smoothed out, I drank more water. I wanted to eat more food, but I was just too tired. Even as I sucked at the bottle, my eyes were falling shut again. And every time they did, there it was . . .

The compound. The barracks. The hand on my shoulder. The face of the guard. His angry eyes. His mouth opening to shout . . .

I climbed wearily back into the front seat. I didn't say anything to Mike. I didn't have the energy. He was silent too, completely focused on pushing the Jeep through the mud that gripped the tires and the rain that lashed the windshield.

I turned on to my side again, resting my head against the seat back. The rain pounded on the roof of the Jeep. The thunder growled like an angry dog, further away than before. We were getting past the storm, I thought.

I let my eyes close as the Jeep bounded and slid . . .

The compound. The barracks. The hand on my shoulder . . .

Just before I fell asleep again, there was a jolt under me. I heard Mike let out a grunt of triumph. Suddenly, the ride smoothed out. Dimly I realized we must have gotten out of the wilderness. We must have made it back on to the pavement, back on to the road.

But I was too exhausted to look and find out for sure. I just wanted sleep – needed sleep.

And I needed to find my way back into the past again. To find out what finally happened . . .

Chapter Twenty

A Very Bad Dream

I heard a footstep behind me. I turned. The guard had completed his patrol and reached the fence. He now started walking back across the compound. He was headed my way.

I was in the past again, in the darkness outside the lighted barracks. Part of me knew I was still, in fact, in the Jeep, dreaming. But, as the moments passed, that part of me started to dissolve. The past enveloped me. I was there completely . . .

I turned away from the guard again, back to the barracks. Prince's voice drifted out to me from inside.

'. . . the Great Death will not be stopped. The basic elements are already in place. Come what may, it will ring in the devil's new year. I will make sure of it personally, if I have to.'

I glanced over my shoulder. The guard kept coming toward me.

'What do you mean everything is in place?' Sherman asked.

'It will be.'

'What about the CO device?'

'It's being acquired from the Russians. The arrangements are progressing.'

'When? When will we have it?'

'Soon.'

'How much?'

'Six canisters.'

'Six . . .'

'It's more than enough. Six canisters can be carried by a single man. So nothing will stop it, even if it comes down to me alone.'

I heard Waylon let out what sounded like a curse in a foreign language.

But I was out of time. I had to get back to my barracks, back into my bed before the guard reached me, before Prince knew I had slipped out to spy on him.

I turned to move away from the building. But, before I could, a hand grabbed me by the shoulder.

My head came around fast. It was the guard. He must've spotted me, hurried quietly over the final distance. All at once, he was standing over me, clutching me hard.

He was a large man with dark olive skin. His sunken eyes burned brightly with excitement and rage under his black beret. I saw his teeth flash as his mouth opened to shout for help.

But before he could, my hand shot out and clutched his throat, cutting off the shout before it could escape him. He moved to tear my hand away, but I was too quick for him. I grabbed him by the shoulder, kicked my leg up behind him and then swiftly swept it in toward myself, knocking his leg out from under him. At the same time, I put my weight behind the hand on his throat, pushing him so that, when he lost the prop of his leg, he went flying backwards. He dropped down to the ground hard and I went down on top of him, still choking off his cry.

My karate training had taught me where to apply the pressure to cut off the blood supply to his brain. He struggled for only a moment, then he was unconscious. He had never made a sound.

He wouldn't be out long though. In a few seconds, a minute at most, he would be awake again. I had to get out of here. But where? Should I run for it? Try to get out of the compound? Or should I go back to my barracks? The guard would find me, accuse me. I would have to call him a liar. I'd already heard that Prince didn't trust me. Could I convince him to believe me instead of his own guard?

As I hesitated, trying to think what to do, I heard the voices inside again.

'Did you hear something?' That was Waylon.

Then Sherman: 'No. Not a thing.'

'What was it?' said Prince.

'I thought . . .' Waylon began.

Quickly, I dragged the unconscious guard toward the

building. I managed to get into the darkness under the wall, out of sight, just as Waylon's figure appeared above me at the window. The light from the building threw his shadow on to the ground in front of me. I looked up and saw him, peering out, searching for any disturbance.

I heard Prince speak from inside the room, 'Do you see anything?'

A long pause as Waylon surveyed the compound. 'No,' he said, drawing out the word uncertainly. 'No, it was probably nothing.'

But he didn't move. He stayed where he was at the window, looking out. So there I was, pinned against the wall of the barracks. If I tried to break back to my own barracks now, Waylon would spot me at once.

I crouched down, holding the guard by his shirt, hoping he wouldn't revive too quickly.

'As I was saying,' Prince went on. 'The point is this – you can see here – the route is set. We have agents at the entrances and exits to insure everything goes smoothly. This is the great and final mission of the Homelanders.'

'But then, why jeopardize it with all these smaller attacks?' I heard Sherman ask. 'I mean, this assassination – won't it make them tighten security?'

'Let them,' said Prince. I could almost hear him shrug. 'The more they try to defend themselves, the more terrified they'll be when they find we can move anywhere, strike anywhere we choose.'

The unconscious guard stirred in my hand. He let out a

low groan. I glanced down at him, but his eyes were still closed, his mouth still hanging open.

I looked up. Waylon was still there above me, watchful, at the window.

Now Prince spoke again. I could hear the smile in his voice. I could picture it: that self-satisfied smile. I could hear the self-satisfied arrogance in his voice, too. 'America is a soft country, ripe for destruction. They are rich and isolated and they think the world is all like them, concerned with nothing but supermarkets and electronics and television shows. They think there is nothing that can't be talked out, that can't be solved peacefully or by passing a few dollars back and forth.'

'Freedom makes people decadent,' said Waylon scornfully. He still hadn't moved from his place at the window.

'Exactly,' Prince went on. 'When you attack Americans, they don't make themselves stronger, they make themselves weaker. They say to themselves, "Oh, if only we are nicer to our enemies, they will see how wonderful we are and come to love us. They will stop being angry at us. They will be nice too and watch TV with us and go to the mall and leave us alone." They don't understand that this is warfare in the name of God, warfare to the death. Two ways of life, two ways of looking at the world that can't be reconciled. One must live and the other must perish.'

Now the unconscious guard shifted on the ground. His eyes remained closed, but he lifted his hand and rubbed at his face as if to bring himself around. I had to do something. Now. Fast. But what?

Prince said, 'They are weary of war, but war is what we live for. They are afraid of death, but death is what we love.' I heard a chair move as if someone had stood up. 'When we hit them again, so hard, right there, right where we hit them so hard before . . . I promise you, what is left of their will to fight will collapse utterly.'

What did he mean, *right there*? Right where? I had to find out.

Just then, Waylon turned away from the window. He moved back into the room, out of sight.

It was my chance, my only chance to find out more. Without even thinking, I let go of the guard. I grabbed hold of the windowsill. I pulled myself up until I could peer over the edge and into the lighted room.

I caught a glimpse – a single glimpse – of the scene inside. The three men in the cramped office. Prince sitting at the desk with the laptop on it. Sherman across from him. Waylon standing over him, with his hands clasped behind his back.

Just a glimpse. I hardly had a chance to take in what I was seeing. Then . . .

'Help me! Help!'

The guard had regained consciousness! He was sitting up. He was shouting.

'Help me! Help!'

I let go of the windowsill. I dropped down to the earth. I leapt on top of the screaming guard, punched him once, hard, fast, to daze him again. I stripped his automatic weapon off

153

his shoulder. And I took off, gun in hand, sprinting away from the building.

I didn't get far.

Two things happened at once. I heard Waylon shout behind me: 'West!'

Then I was blinded with bright light. The guards in the towers had turned their spotlights on me. The next moment, the ground around me was riddled with gunfire, the bullets breaking up the hard-packed dirt of the compound, sending up a cloud of dust. They weren't trying to hit me. If they had, I would've been dead then and there. But the gunfire pinned me to the spot, so that I couldn't run forward. And when I turned to run back, I saw three guards charging at me, their guns lowered.

They were shouting:

'Drop the gun!'

'Put the gun down or you're dead!'

'Put it down! Put your hands up!'

Their voices overlapped in a threatening jumble.

I turned this way and that, looking for a way to escape. I saw Waylon – he was in the doorway of the barracks now. His figure was turned to a black shape by the light shining behind him.

Guards were charging at me from every side. Guards – and my fellow trainees as well. Alerted by the shouts and the gunfire, they came rushing out of their barracks, surrounding me.

For a moment, the guards stopped shouting and there was

a strange silence as if everyone was waiting to find out what would happen next. Pinned in the spotlight beams from the tower, I looked from one guard to another, clutching my gun.

'I would put the weapon down if I were you, Mr West.' This was Prince. He was in the doorway now, too. He had pushed past Waylon and stood in front of him. His voice was soft and calm. 'You have only a second to decide, you know. Then I'll give the order to kill you. I'll count to one,' he said. 'One.'

I had no choice. I threw the AK to the earth. I put my hands up. I was caught.

One of the guards rushed forward to confiscate the weapon.

Prince came walking toward me, casually, in no hurry. Waylon came behind him and Sherman came out of the barracks now too and joined them. Another moment, and Prince stood directly in front of me with Waylon on one side of him and Sherman on the other. I had a moment to feel how strange it was to see Sherman there, my high school history teacher, out in the middle of this murderous place. It was as if my two lives – my normal, everyday past, and this insane nightmare of a present – had come crashing together. Sherman was the link between them.

Prince smiled at me, his bright, ferocious and intelligent eyes gleaming with the glow of the spotlights. Every slick black hair was in place, his goatee neatly trimmed. He was wearing a dark suit and a white shirt, open at the neck, as if he'd just come home from working at the bank and was relaxing after a long day.

'I caught him outside your window.' This was the guard I had knocked out. He emerged from the shadows of the barracks, rubbing his throat.

Prince glanced at him, then back at me. 'Outside my window,' he repeated softly.

'He was listening,' said the guard.

'I was just . . .' I started, but I fell silent when Prince lifted his hand.

'Don't insult my intelligence please, Mr West.' He studied me a moment. 'I don't suppose you care to tell me who you're working for?'

'I'm working for you,' I insisted. 'I came here to work for you. I was just coming to talk to Waylon about . . .'

But again, he lifted his hand and I stopped talking. What was the use? I didn't sound convincing, even to myself.

Prince examined me for a long quiet moment. Then he glanced at Waylon – casually, as if he were about to tell him to send out for a pizza so we could all share a late-night snack.

Instead he said, 'Torture him until he tells you everything. Then kill him.'

Chapter Twenty-one

The Final Piece

When I woke up, the rain had stopped. It was almost dusk.

Blinking, confused, I sat up on the Jeep's passenger seat. I looked out through the windshield.

A long highway ran before us through grassy hills to a darkening sky. There were a few cars and trucks ahead of us and behind us, but not many. Traffic was light and we were moving quickly. There were still lots of clouds in the sky but they were drifting apart now. Patches of blue and rays of slanting sunlight were appearing between them. There was nothing left of the great storm.

For a dazed moment, I couldn't remember where I was or how I had gotten here. Then the violence of the storm – the rain, the lightning, the thunder – and the danger of the day – the mad escape, the guards, the prisoners, the cops – slowly came back to me: broken pieces that fit themselves together inside my head like some kind of automated jigsaw.

I turned and saw Mike behind the wheel. I remembered

how he had come to find me in the middle of nowhere, in the middle of the rain.

Mike glanced over at me, his faint, ironic smile hidden by the big black moustache. 'Rise and shine, chucklehead,' he said.

My mouth was dry. I swallowed hard. 'Mike . . . I remember . . .'

He turned serious right away. 'Remember what?'

'Everything,' I said slowly. 'Or most of it . . .' It was still like a dream, still putting itself together out of half-remembered fragments. 'I was in the Homelanders' compound. I snuck out of my room in the middle of the night. I was eavesdropping outside a barracks, trying to hear Prince's plans. That's when they caught me, strapped me to that chair. They had a couple of their goons torture me for information, to find out who I was working for . . .' I looked over at Mike as the whole memory came to me. He looked out the windshield at the road, his face expressionless, his thoughts impossible to read. 'I knew I couldn't stand the pain forever. I was going to tell them – about Waterman and the others, our plan to stop them. So I cracked the implant Waterman had had put inside my mouth. It released a drug that erased my memory – everything about the year before. Maybe I shouldn't have done it, but the pain was terrible and I just didn't think—'

'No, no – that was smart,' said Mike. 'That was the right thing to do.'

'Maybe if I had toughed it out, maybe if I'd been stronger . . .'

'Don't be a chucklehead, chucklehead,' he said. 'No one can stand up to that kind of pain forever. Not Chuck Norris, not John Wayne, not me, not you, not anyone. You did the only thing you could do. You erased the information so they couldn't get at it. That's why Waterman gave you that stuff to begin with. He understood.'

Slowly, I nodded. If anyone knew about being tough, Mike was the guy. Never mind Chuck Norris and John Wayne. If Mike said he couldn't stand it then I guess no one could.

'So that's the story,' I said. 'That's why it seemed like I went to sleep in my own bed one night and then woke up being tortured, wanted by the police, all that. I'd destroyed my own memory to keep from giving up my friends. But now it's back. My memory, my life – it's back. I remember everything right up until the moment they caught me. And I remember something else too.'

Mike glanced at me again, lifting one black eyebrow in a question.

'Prince said the Great Death would ring in the devil's new year,' I told him. 'And then he said it would be "right there, right where we hit them before." '

'What's that mean? The World Trade Center? New York City?'

'New York, yeah. At least I think so . . .' Something teased the corner of my memory, but I couldn't quite reach it. 'I'm almost sure.'

'New York at New Year's,' Mike murmured. 'With, like, a billion people in Times Square waiting for the ball to drop.'

I looked out the window at the peaceful hills. My stomach clutched with fear. So many people all together in one place.

'Tomorrow night,' I said. 'One day away.'

'Well . . .' Mike said. 'At least there'll be a whole lot of security around New York on New Year's Eve.'

I shook my head. 'I think that's what Prince started with. That's what they were doing the whole time we were in training. Planting Homelanders – native-born Americans – in places that would help them infiltrate all that security. Maybe they're even part of the security system itself. That's why Prince sounded so sure of himself. That's what he had up his sleeve all along.'

Mike made no response. He only said, 'There's our exit.'

He guided the Jeep off the highway to the ramp. We came to a little town in the middle of nowhere, surrounded by hills. We passed a small strip of gas stations and restaurants. Then we left the town behind. We were on a small lane winding more deeply into the rolling grasslands. As the car meandered into nowhere, the last light of day faded into night.

The last night before the new year, before the Great Death.

We were on a lonely road – not a light anywhere. I turned to Mike. I could only just make out his steady features in the green glow from the dashboard.

'Where are we going?' I asked him.

'We're almost there,' he said.

'But—'

'After you told me you were going to join the prisoners in

their escape, I contacted every Special Ops guy I knew, every undercover source I had. I sent out the word through every network I have that I needed to get in touch with Rose.'

'Rose? Did you? Did you get in touch with him?'

'No,' Mike said. 'I didn't have to. Rose got in touch with me.' He glanced over at me. 'He sent me to find you. They still need you, chucklehead.'

He lifted his chin toward the windshield. I turned and followed his gesture.

We had come off the road now. We were bumping down a dirt lane. Up ahead, in the glow of the headlights, I could see an empty field, the grass cut low. In the middle of the field there was a grassless strip of hard-packed dirt. It was a landing strip. A small Cessna airplane was sitting at one end of it.

And Rose was leaning against the fuselage, waiting for us.

Chapter Twenty-two

Night Flight

'Well, you're out of the frying pan,' Rose told me. 'But now you're really in the fire.'

His voice came over my headset as the Cessna moved through the night sky. The stars drifted slowly past at the windows. Sporadic lights appeared below and went slowly by.

I was sitting up front in the passenger seat. The headset blocked out the noise from the pounding engine, but that pound still surrounded me, surrounded everything. Rose's voice was small and distant at the center of that rhythm, but I could hear his words clearly.

'Washington has shut our mission down completely,' Rose went on. 'Shut us down and shut us out. I was afraid even to try to get you protection for your escape, afraid they'd alert the guards – and that the guards would shoot you. The best I could do is post Mike out there with an off-road vehicle and the best surveillance equipment I could find, so he could track you whenever you made your run for it. But, all the same, you're just plain lucky you got out of Abingdon alive. You have no idea how much danger you were in.'

The pilot glanced over from the seat beside me. He was a small, thin man named Patel. He had black hair, large eyes and an easy-going smile. When he heard Rose's words, he jogged his eyebrows at me, up and down, comically, as if potentially getting killed in a prison break was just some big adventure. Then, with a quick grin, he faced forward. He flew the plane low over the dark territory beneath. I guessed that he was intentionally staying below any controlled airspace. Now and then, we heard a voice from a control tower somewhere, but Patel never answered. He flew the plane without a word.

Rose was sitting right behind me, right next to Mike in the cramped rear seats. His voice continued in my ear. 'Already, since the escape, Abingdon has started to come apart at the seams. The guards are totally corrupt, some bought off by the Nazis, some by the Islamists. That guy Dunbar was running some kind of drug ring. Even the Warden was in on it. The whole place was a cesspool.'

'Gee,' I said, 'and it seemed so pleasant on the surface.'

I heard Mike chuckle. Rose didn't chuckle. He wasn't the chuckling sort.

'So, like I said, you're out of the frying pan,' he went on. 'But you're no better off. Worse, maybe, if it comes to that. Now the cops are hunting for you all over the place. Washington denies you ever worked for them. And, when I try to pass on your warnings, my bosses won't believe me.'

'They won't believe you about the Great Death?'

'They say they've got any number of threats centered around New Year's Eve and that security is as tight as it can be everywhere. Even if they wanted to, there's no way to amp it up any further.'

'But Prince was counting on that from the beginning.'

'He must've been, if he's planning to go through with it.'

'So where does that leave us?'

I heard Rose sigh over the headset. 'Alone, pretty much. Or, at least, if we're going to get some help, if we're going to get anyone to take us seriously, we've got to figure out just what exactly Prince is planning. Without that, I can't call in reinforcements. There's nowhere to call them to.'

'But I'm pretty sure it's going to take place in New York. Isn't that enough? Couldn't we tell them—?'

'You're "pretty sure," ' said Rose sourly. 'That's my point. And no, it's not enough for you to be pretty sure of something or even to remember something. We have to prove it, if we're going to get any action.'

I rolled that over in my mind for a moment as the plane moved smoothly over a small town. With the town's street lights and house lights glittering in the night, it looked like some kind of jewel lying on a black background.

'So what are we going to do?' I said finally. 'We've only got twenty-four hours left – if that.'

It was a moment before he answered – so long, in fact, I looked over my shoulder at him. Then he said, 'Well, for one thing, we've got to use the information we already have and try to pinpoint exactly where Prince is planning to go. And for another thing . . .' He didn't finish the sentence.

The plane bucked and wavered as it flew through a pocket of rough air. The stars dipped and rose at the windows.

'What?' I said finally. 'For another thing, what?' This time, when I looked back at him, I saw Rose and Mike exchange a glance.

'We're hoping you can help us, Charlie,' Rose said then. 'We're hoping you'll remember something that will help us.'

'Well, I'll tell you whatever I can . . .'

They glanced at each other again.

After that, no one said anything for a while. I sat there, staring out the window, thinking back over the memories that had returned to me, especially the memory of that conversation I'd overheard inside the barracks: Prince and Waylon and Sherman plotting out the Great Death. I had this feeling that I was missing something, some essential clue to the exact nature of their plan. I had this feeling there was something I knew that I didn't know I knew.

'What's a CO device?' I asked. 'I heard Prince say they were going to acquire it from the Russians.'

'Yeah, we're checking on that now,' Rose said. 'Is there anything else? Anything else you remember that might help. Something specific about the location of the attack? The time?'

I shook my head. 'Not that I can think of . . .' But again, I had that feeling that there *was* something, something just beyond my memory . . .

Rose fell silent behind me. He sat back in his seat.

The plane trundled on. I tried to think back, page through my memories, but I couldn't think of anything useful.

After a little while, Patel turned to me from the pilot seat. He seemed completely unaffected by our conversation: cheerful and relaxed. He looked like he'd just been waiting for his chance to speak to me.

'I hear you want to be in the Air Force,' he said.

I nodded. 'Yeah, that's right.'

'So you ever pilot a plane before?'

'A couple of times. I took some lessons – you know, taking off and landing – but I never got my license. I never even soloed.'

'Want to fly it now?'

I sat up straight. It was the best offer I'd had in – well, for as long as I could think of. 'Yeah, you kidding? Absolutely!'

Patel let go of the pilot's stick and let me take the co-pilot's control, right in front of me. My feet found the rudders on the floor and my eyes scanned the cockpit's instrument panels, trying to remember which digital readout was which and what they all meant. I followed the track laid out for me on the GPS, turning the plane slightly this way or that, remembering to work the pedals at the same time I turned the yolk.

The feel of the plane came back to me quickly. Soon, I was holding it steady, looking out through the windshield at the sky. It's an almost magical feeling, flying a small plane at night. You feel like you're sailing on a sea of stars. Best of all, for long, good minutes, it took my mind off things, off the heaviness inside me, the dread of what was coming next. It gave me a break from the tension that had tied me in knots for so long, ever since I'd been put in prison. Plus, it was fun.

I had no idea how deadly serious it would be before all this was over.

After a while, Patel took the plane back. 'If it's been a while since you took lessons, I think you better let me land it.'

'Yeah, especially at night,' I said.

The Cessna started to drop down through the darkness. I peered out through the windshield but I didn't see anything ahead of us. I could just make out the darker darkness of the earth beneath the sky. But there was no place to land.

Then, a light gleamed and died. Patel corrected the plane's course and headed toward it. I watched him as he pushed in the throttle, raised the flaps, slowed the plane so that its nose angled down and the plane sank out of the sky.

The light flashed below again and, for a moment, I could make out the shape of a small dirt runway in the middle of an overgrown field, just at the bottom of a small hill. The setting looked familiar to me somehow.

'Where are we?' I said into the headset microphone.

Rose's voice came back to me over the headphones. 'Look to your right.'

I did. At first I couldn't see a thing. Then, against the background of the starry sky, an unmistakeable shape appeared. It was a building, a house, with a large central tower and two smaller towers, one to either side.

It was that quirky mansion that served as Prince's headquarters.

The plane dropped down slowly toward the earth.

Chapter Twenty-three

Reunion

An odd feeling came to me as I walked into that crazy place again. It wasn't exactly a feeling of nostalgia and not exactly déjà vu either. But the halls and rooms with their great curtains and enormous fireplaces and marble statues and staring portraits on the walls and shining knick-knacks everywhere – it all felt familiar to me and I liked that feeling. I liked remembering. I liked having my life back in my mind again.

Rose led the way, up the front porch and through the doors into the great foyer; up the broad stairs and down the thickly carpeted hallway; back to the room that Prince had used for his headquarters.

As I stepped in, I broke into a smile – a tremendously painful smile, I have to say, because my face had stiffened up from all its bruises – but a smile all the same.

There, swiveling around in the high-backed chair where I'd first seen Prince, was Milton One – Waterman's tech guy. He was a youngish guy with a square head, Asian features. They called him Milton One because he was the inventor and operator of Milton Two, a security device that had come in pretty handy to me once not long before. He and all his friends had disappeared when Waterman was killed and I didn't know where they'd gotten to. I'd worried they were dead. I was glad to see Milton One alive. I saluted him and he gave me a big wave hello.

Then I recognized the others. There was Dodger Jim, Waterman's tough muscleman. He was still wearing his Dodgers baseball cap. And there was the crow-faced woman – I never knew her name. She was the one who'd injected me with the antidote that started my memory coming back. They were hovering around Milton One, looking over his shoulder at a small computer he had set up on Prince's enormous desk.

Despite my growing sense of dread, I was glad to see them. After the evil weeks in Abingdon, it was good to be back among allies.

'How goes it?' Rose asked them.

'Well, I have bad news and really bad news,' said Milton One casually. 'Which do you want first?'

'Gimme the bad news,' said Rose. 'Let's build up slowly to the really bad.'

Milton One's voice remained casual, but I could see by the look in his eyes that he was about to tell us something really gnarly. 'Nothing is a hundred per cent certain, but if I were a betting man, I'd put my money on the fact that Prince has secured the device he was after.'

I heard Rose let out a long, weary breath.

'Is that the CO device?' I asked him.

He nodded wearily.

'What is it?'

It was Milton One who answered me. 'CO stands for Cylon Orange. It's a chemical weapon invented in the Soviet Union.'

'When the USSR went down, their small supply of CO disappeared,' Rose said. 'We always figured someone would try to sell it off to some rogue state or bad actors.'

'And now you think Prince has gotten it?'

'Looks that way.'

'Six canisters' worth,' said Milton One.

I remembered hearing Prince's voice from the barracks:

Six canisters . . . It's more than enough. Six canisters can be carried by a single man. So nothing will stop it, even if it comes down to me alone.

'What's it do?' I asked.

'The canisters hold the CO in an inert liquid form. You put them inside a device about the size of a backpack. When the device is activated, it injects an acid into the canisters that turns the CO to a poison gas which is then sprayed out into the air.'

I stood there silent for a moment, trying to get a picture of this in my mind.

Then Rose added, 'The whole point about Cylon Orange is its density. Six canisters is enough to wipe out four city blocks.'

Now everyone was silent. I felt my lips go dry. I felt my

heart beating so hard I thought the others could surely hear it. 'Four city blocks in New York City on New Year's Eve . . .'

'How many people you figure that is?' Mike asked Rose.

Rose tilted his head, considering. 'If it's in Times Square, where the ball drops? I don't know. Could be a million people there. A million, at least.'

I opened my mouth but nothing came out. I couldn't think of what to say. A million people. The Great Death.

'They should shut the city down,' I said finally. 'Cancel the celebration. Block off the bridges and tunnels.'

More silence. Everyone nodded slowly.

Milton One said quietly, 'That's the really bad news.'

We waited for him to go on.

'I've got everything there is now. Every record, every correspondence that wasn't destroyed beyond recovery. There's no data left to mine. And in all of it, I came up with not one clue where Prince is headed. Nothing about the exact nature of his plan, his target . . . Nothing.'

I looked from Milton One to Rose to Mike.

'What's that mean?' I asked them. 'What's that got to do with anything? We know Prince is headed for New York—'

'No, we don't,' said Rose. 'We think he is. You think he is. You sort of remember—'

'I *do* remember.'

'But you don't remember anything definitive, Charlie. It's like I told you. The government has got a dozen threats like this, all the time, especially at holidays. They can't just shut down every city in the country, send everyone into a panic.

Unless we have something more definitive, more certain—'

'But . . .' I started, but the look on his face – the look on his face and Mike's face – made me stop. I knew if there was something to be done, they'd already be doing it.

What happened next was kind of awful. There was this silence. Everyone in the room was just sitting there, standing there, without saying a word. If they were anything like me, they were thinking about those million people in Times Square, Prince, the canisters of gas.

Even if I have to do it on my own, the Great Death will not be stopped.

Standing in that room, I could almost feel the time passing, the night passing, tomorrow coming: New Year's Eve.

The silence stretched out and out, moment after moment. It gave me a terrible sense of hopelessness.

And then – this was the awful part – then I realized everyone was looking at me. That's why they were silent. They were waiting – waiting for me to say something. Something that would help them. Something that would give us a clue, a direction – a chance.

Mike was the one who asked the question out loud: 'Is there anything, Charlie? Anything you might have forgotten? Any memory that might be worth digging up, going over again?'

'What do you mean? I've told you everything I know . . .'

Now it was Rose's turn. 'Do you think it might be worth . . . going back?'

'Going back?'

'In time. In your memory. To see . . .'

I heard a noise from behind the desk: a sharp intake of breath; a muttered complaint. I turned and looked. It was the crow-faced woman. She had straightened up behind the big chair. She was . . . *scowling* is the only word I can think of to describe it.

'This is insane,' she said. 'Tell him.'

I looked from her to Mike and Rose. 'Tell me what?'

Again, Mike and Rose exchanged a glance. Then, as if they'd agreed to it silently, Mike did the talking.

'We're at a dead end, chucklehead. You've heard the danger. If you're right – and we think you are – we're looking at a disaster beyond anything we can imagine. In fact, that's the problem: no one can imagine it. No one's going to pull the trigger and shut down New York on the basis of our guesswork.'

'When it's over,' Rose added bitterly, 'there'll be hearings and finger-pointing and political maneuvering and blame. And none of it will make a bit of difference to the dead.'

'Yeah, I get it,' I said. 'But what do you want me to do?'

'If,' said Mike, holding the word, emphasizing the word. 'If you think there's something left in your brain, something we haven't gotten to, something that could help . . . we could give you another dose of the stuff they gave you before.'

'It's insane,' the crow-faced woman blurted out angrily. 'A second dose of this stuff could kill him. It could destroy his brain, put him in a vegetative state for the rest of his life. And it might not even work. We've never tried it or tested it on anyone a second time. We haven't dared. It's insane.'

She stopped. She turned away.

Mike said, 'She's right, Charlie. It's powerful stuff. You already know that. I wouldn't want you to do it for no reason. But if you think there might be something you missed, something worth remembering . . .'

His voice trailed off. I stared at him. I stared at Rose. Then, after a second, I lifted my hand to my face and pinched the bridge of my nose, squeezing my eyes shut. I was thinking about that moment – that moment in the Jeep with Mike when something – some memory – had teased at the corner of my mind. It had happened in the plane, too. There *was* something – something I knew but didn't know I knew. Something I'd seen but couldn't quite remember . . .

I felt everyone's eyes on me as I walked across the colorful rug, past the gilded chairs, to the high window. I looked out beyond the thick drapery, saw my own bruised and exhausted expression reflected on the dark pane of glass. I looked out through the image of my own hollow eyes into the night beyond.

It might kill him. It might destroy his brain. Put him into a vegetative state for the rest of his life.

I drew a deep breath. *A million people*, I thought. More than twice the population of my home town.

And there was something. Something. What was it? What had I seen or overheard in the compound, in the barracks?

I remembered Prince's voice:

When we hit them again, so hard, right there, right where we hit them so hard before . . .

I remembered crouching beneath the barracks' window with the unconscious guard slowly coming around.

The point is this – you can see here – the route is set. We have agents at the entrances and exits to insure everything goes smoothly. This is the great and final mission of the Homelanders . . .

I felt my body go taut. 'Wait,' I said.

I turned around. They were all looking at me: Rose and Mike, Milton One and Dodger Jim – and the crow-faced woman, she was looking at me too now.

'There is something,' I told them. 'Only . . .'

I looked at him helplessly. 'I'm not sure what it is. When I was eavesdropping on the barracks, listening to Prince make his plans, he said to the others – to Waylon and Mr Sherman – he said, "You can see here – the route is set."'

Rose never showed much emotion, but he showed some now. At least, he licked his lips and took a half step toward me. For him, that was a sign of wild excitement.

'What did he mean "see here"? See where?'

'That's just it,' I said. 'That's why I got caught. I realized he must be showing them something – a map or something – so I grabbed hold of the windowsill and chinned my way up so I could peek in.'

'And?' said Rose. 'What did you see?'

I opened my mouth but nothing came out. There was nothing to say. I shook my head.

'Come on, chucklehead,' said Mike. 'There had to be something.'

I stared down at the floor. I thought back to the room inside the barracks. 'I only saw it for a single second before the guard started to scream for help,' I murmured.

'Think, Charlie,' said Rose. 'What did you see?'

'The room. Prince. Waylon. Sherman. The desk.' My head came up, fast. 'The laptop! The laptop turned around to face the others. That must've been what he was showing them.'

'Did you see it? Did you see the screen?' said Rose:

I tried to think back, but in the end I could only spread my hands. 'I saw it but . . . it was so fast . . .'

There was another awful silence – everyone looking at me – but I felt one stare more than the others.

I turned to her – to the crow-faced woman – the woman who had injected the drug that had sent me into paroxysms of agonizing pain – and into the past so that I could begin to recover my lost memories.

'I never knew your name,' I said. 'Nobody ever told me.'

'Farber,' she said quietly. 'Dr Judith Farber.' She averted her eyes as if she couldn't bear to look at me.

'Do you think it might work?' I asked her. 'Do you think I could go back – to that specific moment, that specific memory?'

She couldn't meet my eyes. 'Early on, when we were first developing the drug,' she said, 'there was some evidence that, with experience, you might be able to control it to some degree – just like thinking back to a specific time, only . . .'

'Only more powerful,' I said, 'because of the drug.'

She looked at me – forced herself to look at me, I think. She said, 'I don't know. I don't know what would happen.' She looked around at the others as if she were appealing to them. 'Nobody knows.'

No one answered her. No one said a word.

'If I could go back,' I told her, 'if I could look into that room again . . . I might see the laptop again, I might see what I saw but can't remember. It's possible, isn't it?'

'Oh, it's possible,' said Dr Farber. Her tone was almost desperate. She stared an appeal at Milton One and Dodger Jim, then at Mike and Rose, and finally at me. 'It's possible but . . .'

'But it might kill me. Or worse.'

She nodded. 'Or worse. Yes.'

After that, nothing but silence all around. I turned back to the window. I stared into my own face again and through my reflection again into the darkness. I could say that I wasn't afraid. I could say I trusted in God. And I did trust in God. But I was afraid, too.

A million people, I thought.

I faced the others. Mike looked at me and I looked at Mike and I'm pretty sure I knew exactly what he was thinking: *You do what you gotta do, chucklehead. You never surrender and you do what you have to do.*

'I want to call Beth first,' I told them. 'Just in case, you know. I want a chance to say goodbye.'

Chapter Twenty-four

To Say Goodbye

Mike and Milton One took me into a bedroom – another one of these elaborate bedrooms in this crazy house. There was a four-poster bed all draped with heavy curtains and heavy curtains on the windows, and tables everywhere cluttered with shiny knick-knacks and chiming clocks.

Mike grabbed all the knick-knacks from one table in a single big arm-load. He carried them to the bed and dumped them with a ringing clatter on the lacy bedspread.

Milton One set a laptop on the cleared table. 'I've got the signal scrambled through about three different servers,' he told me, 'but I wouldn't stay on with her more than ten minutes if I were you. The cops are looking for you and may be monitoring her line. And Prince will know you escaped. You're the one person who might know enough to catch up with him, so, even though he hasn't got a lot of manpower left, he's sure to be looking out for you, waiting for a chance to send someone after you. Like I said, I've got it fixed to confuse a trace but if you stay on too long . . . Well, ten minutes – tops.'

I nodded. Milton One walked out of the room. Mike hesitated.

'What?' I said.

My old sensei didn't say anything. He just lifted his right fist – the karate sign of power. Then he covered it with his left hand – the karate sign of restraint. Then, holding his hands like that, he gave a short sharp bow in my direction – the karate token of respect.

Then he walked out of the room, closing the door behind him.

I waited a few minutes. Just a few. I wanted to be sure my emotions were under control. There are people, I know, who say guys shouldn't control their emotions, that they should just express them any time they want. I don't agree. There's a time to be emotional, sure, but there're also plenty of times when it's good to keep your emotions in check. I wanted Beth to know I loved her, but I didn't want her to see I was afraid, because I didn't want her to be afraid.

When I could, I pulled up some fancy French-looking chair and sat down in front of the laptop. I remembered the system my pal Josh had set up for communications. I used it now.

A long tone came out of the laptop's speakers. Then there was Beth's voice:

'Charlie?'

It was another second or two before the video came on.

179

Then there she was, looking into the screen. Her hair falling in curls around her cheeks made her look like one of those cameos my mother sometimes wears. Her blue eyes were gazing right at me and there was an expectant smile on her lips. Then I guess she saw me at about the same time I saw her, because she kind of gave a little gasp and put her hands over her mouth.

I know I should have been glad to see her. All this time, every day, every minute, I'd missed her more than I could even bear to think about. So I should've been glad. But I wasn't. Or, that is, I felt a weird mix of soaring gladness and plunging sorrow all at the same time. The sight of her made my heart clench inside me because I had a very strong feeling that I was never going to see her again.

I didn't show any of that though. I just smiled at her – a big bright smile. 'Hey, Beth,' I said.

'Look at your face,' Beth said. 'Your poor face.'

Without thinking, I reached up to touch it and flinched at the pain. 'Tough place, Abingdon,' I told her.

She nodded. 'We heard the news here about how you escaped again,' she answered softly. 'The lawyers say you've ruined your chances for an appeal. The police say you're going to get hurt if you don't turn yourself in. I don't care what anyone says: I'm glad you're out of there.'

'I'm glad too, Beth.'

She peered into the screen. She looked . . . I'm not sure what the word is to describe her. She looked like she trusted me – that's it.

180

She said, 'What's going to happen now, Charlie?'

What could I tell her? 'I don't know – not exactly, anyway. But one way or another, Beth, this is almost over. There's just one more bad guy out there . . .'

'And you have to fight him, because you're the good guy. I know.'

'That's the way it works, yeah.'

'Is it dangerous?' she asked. Then, right away, she said, 'I guess that's a stupid question. It must be really dangerous or you wouldn't have risked calling me.'

I managed a laugh. 'You're too smart for me.'

'And don't you forget it, Charlie.'

I looked into her soft eyes. That sweet face. It was amazing, I thought, how well I remembered the smell of her hair. It was amazing how often the scent of it had reached me in my prison cell as if she had been sitting on my cot, watching over me while I slept, and had only left a moment before I woke up.

'After this,' she said, 'they'll see the truth. I know they will. They won't send you back to prison this time.'

I didn't argue with her. 'I hope not,' was all I said.

'I couldn't stand thinking about you in there,' she told me. 'I tried not to show it.'

'You did a good job,' I lied.

'But I couldn't stand it. It was killing me.'

Yeah, me too, I thought. But what I said was, 'I'm sorry, Beth. I'm really sorry for putting you through all this.'

She gave a quick shake of her head. 'No. Don't say that.

You're not sorry. I'm not sorry either. If I had known at the start this was what you were doing, I would have told you to do it. I love you because you're the person who will do it.'

'OK,' I said. 'I'm glad. Tell you the truth, I don't really care why you love me, as long as you find a reason. Although I was kind of hoping it was cause I'm just so incredibly hot.'

'It isn't.'

'Yeah, I didn't think so.'

She smiled, but a tear dropped over the edge of her eye and rolled down her cheek. She brushed it away quickly. 'I know what you're doing, Charlie. Don't think you're fooling me, OK? I know exactly what you're doing.'

'Oh yeah? What am I doing?'

'You're calling to say goodbye. You're thinking you're going to get killed out there so you're calling so we can talk to each other one last time.'

'Is that so?'

'Yes. Only you're wrong. You're not going to get killed.'

'No?' I said.

'No. You're not. You're going to find whoever you have to find and do whatever you have to do and then . . .' Her voice broke. She put her hand over her eyes for a moment – only for a moment. Then she looked at me again, tears streaming down her cheeks. 'And then you're coming back. You hear me? When you're done, when it's all done, you're coming back to me and to your mom and dad and to Josh and Rick and Miler and everybody. And that's how it's going to be. OK?'

'Yeah,' my voice was hoarse. I could hardly get the words out. 'Sure, Beth. That's how it's going to be.'

'Good,' she said, using her palm to swipe the tears off her cheeks. 'As long as we understand one another.'

'I understand,' I said. 'You're with me every second, Beth.'

'Yes,' she answered. 'I am.'

I lifted my hand. I put it to the computer screen. She lifted her hand and put it to the screen on her side.

We sat like that – in silence. Time seemed to stand still. Seemed to – but it didn't. When I came back to myself, I realized we'd been on the line too long.

'Listen . . .' I said finally.

'I know,' Beth said, her voice almost a whisper. 'You have to go.'

'I wish . . .'

'Me too,' she said.

My hand was still half lifted to the screen. But now I lowered it. My fingers curled into a fist and I pressed the fist against my heart. My way of telling her again, one last time, that she was with me still, with me always.

She did the same with her hand.

'See you,' I said.

'See you,' she said.

Then I shut down the connection.

Chapter Twenty-five

One Last Memory

They wanted to strap me down, but I wouldn't let them. I was tired of feeling trapped and helpless. Tired of being pushed around and told what to do. This was my choice, my decision. I didn't need any straps.

I rolled up my sleeve and held it out to Dr Farber. 'Just do it,' I told her.

I was sitting in the big chair behind the desk. Milton One and Dodger Jim were standing near me. Mike was leaning against the desk, his arms crossed on his chest, watching me. Rose was standing at the window, staring out at the night.

Dr Farber lifted the hypodermic. She took a breath.

'Isn't this where you're supposed to say it won't hurt a bit?' I asked her.

She tried to smile, but didn't do a very good job. She leaned forward and pressed the hypodermic's needle against my arm.

I didn't want to watch. I looked at Mike. He winked at me. I winked back.

The needle went into me.

I thought I was ready for the pain. I wasn't. With all the memory attacks I'd experienced, I thought I'd been through it before and could take it. But this was worse – much worse – than it had ever been. For what must have been a minute, but seemed like days, I lay in thrashing contortions on the floor. I heard myself screaming in mindless agony.

Then – thank God – I felt as if I was plunging out of my own agonized body, plunging into a darkening whirlpool of time, and my own screams slowly faded away into ever receding echoes.

Now, at last, the echoes faded too. I fell from the whirlpool into empty space. That's what it seemed like, anyway. It seemed like I was dropping down and down and down through a vast empty space whose only limit was the past spread out beneath me. Moments of the past played themselves out far below as I tumbled toward them, watching. I caught glimpses of my whole life as it seemed to replay itself all in a single moment. There was me and Alex Hauser as little kids on a baseball field . . . Me as a miniature yellow belt in Sensei Mike's karate class for children . . . Me at the dinner table with my mom and dad and my sister, Amy, rolling her eyes at some new horror-of-horrors that she'd experienced that day in school . . . Me and my friends clowning around at our lunch table in the cafeteria . . . Me with Beth . . . Me slipping into the car next to Waterman to hear what he wanted me to do . . . Me with Alex again, teenagers now, arguing in my mom's car before he stormed off into the park where Mr Sherman stabbed him to death . . . My trial for his murder . . . the Homelanders' compound . . .

There was so much time flashing before my eyes as I spun and tumbled down. At first, I couldn't think. My mind was clouded with confusion. Where was I? Where was I going? What was happening to my body? Was that me I could still hear screaming in the far distance? Was I dying? Was this what the end looked like?

But then, I remembered . . . not the past . . . the present . . . the Great Death . . . New Year's Eve . . . No time for fear and confusion. No time. No time.

I fought my rising panic down. I forced myself to focus. I had done this a million times before – in sparring matches, in belt tests, in fights with killers. I knew how to focus when I had to and I had to now.

One memory. That's what I needed. I needed to find one memory and fall into it. I focused my mind with all the energy I had . . .

There it was. I saw it below me: the compound; the barracks; the unconscious guard on the ground . . .

I guided my fall toward it.

If you've ever jumped off a really high diving board, you will know what it felt like then. That plunge where you think that any second you should hit the water, but the second passes and you're still going down and down, and your stomach starts to rise inside you and then . . .

Then I was there. I had done it. I was in the compound. I was underneath the barracks' window. The guard was unconscious beside me. Waylon was standing at the window above me. Prince's voice was drifting out to me.

They are weary of war, but war is what we live for. They are afraid of death, but death is what we love.

The guard stirred on the ground, waking.

Then Waylon moved away from the window. And I leapt up. I grabbed hold of the sill. I lifted myself. I looked in.

It was one of those weird double moments. I was in the past but I was in the present, too. I knew I was lying on the floor in the weird mansion screaming in agony. And I knew I was in the Homelanders' compound. I knew the guard was about to cry for help. I was about to be caught. But now – right now – there was this one moment – looking in the window . . .

Look! I thought desperately. *Look!*

I looked.

There was Sherman, Prince, Waylon, the table, the laptop. The laptop.

Look, Charlie! What's on the laptop?

'*I see it!*' I shouted. '*I see it, I see it!*'

Then, like an enormous, monstrous paw made of fire rising up from the bottom of the earth, breaking through the earth's surface to grab me, pain – pain like nothing I had ever known before – wrapped itself around me, closed its flaming fingers tight.

'No!' I shouted.

I tried to fight it off, but it was no use. It was irresistible. It dragged me off the windowsill. It dragged me down and down, out of the compound, out of time, out of memory, down into an all-consuming agony like nothing else.

I have to tell them! I thought. *Don't let me die. Please. Not yet. Mike. Rose. I have to tell them what I saw!*

It was the last sensible thought I had. After that, there was nothing – nothing at all – but falling and pain and blackness.

PART IV

Chapter Twenty-six

All There Is

I saw a blue sky. The sun like a medallion. I felt myself floating upward into the light. For a weirdly peaceful moment, I actually thought I was dead and headed elsewhere.

Then the world contracted in a spasm of pain. I flinched, my eyes shut, my teeth gritted. No, I wasn't dead. This hurt too much to be anything but life!

The gripping pain slowly passed. I opened my eyes.

I was lying on a four-poster bed in a room of high windows. The bed curtains had been pulled aside – so had the window curtains. The skyscape through the pane filled my vision. Then I turned away, looked around me.

I was in that bedroom again, the room where I'd talked to Beth. Heavy curtains, colorful rugs, knick-knacks glittering everywhere, clocks ticking. Clocks . . . The light . . . It must be morning now . . . No – later. The sun was low but midway through its transit, as in a winter noon. I stared at a small domed clock sitting on one of the many end-tables. After twelve . . .

I sat up fast – too fast. For a moment, I was almost overcome by dizziness and nausea. I fought it off and pushed the bedcovers aside. I stumbled to my feet.

'It's all right,' said a woman's voice behind me.

Startled, I turned. There was Dr Farber, sitting in a chair in the corner. A giant portrait hung above her of some rich guy in a three-piece suit. Beneath the picture, she looked small and fragile. Her sharp, crow-like face was gray, her eyes sunken. She was exhausted.

'You made it,' she said. 'How do you feel?'

'Fine, but where . . . ?' I began, but another wave of dizziness went over me, and I sat down hard on the edge of the bed.

'They're all downstairs,' Dr Farber said quietly. 'They're getting ready.'

'Ready . . .'

'You slept the night and most of the morning, Charlie,' she said. 'For a while there, I wasn't sure you were going to come back at all.'

I tried to take it in. 'All night . . . The morning . . . It must be . . .'

'It's New Year's Eve.'

'New Year's . . .'

Urgency cleared my mind, washed my nausea and dizziness away in an instant. I was on my feet in a moment. I suddenly realized I was undressed, wearing nothing but underwear.

Reading my mind, Dr Farber pointed to a gilded chair

against the wall. There were clothes folded on it. 'Those are clean.'

Jeans. A T-shirt. A sweatshirt. A baseball jacket. I pulled them on quickly.

Then I looked at Dr Farber. She continued to gaze at me, weary but glad – glad to see me alive, I think.

'Do you remember what happened last night?' she asked me.

I thought about it. I did remember: the injection, the renewed memories.

I see it!

'Did I do it?' I asked her. 'Did I remember anything useful?'

She nodded wearily. 'You did it, Charlie. You remembered – and you told us about it.'

I shook my head. The night before was a blur.

'Rose and Mike,' said Dr Farber. 'They have it all. They know what they need to know.'

'Where . . . ?' I began.

'They're in the kitchen,' Dr Farber said.

Like everything else in the mansion, the kitchen was huge. There was a high ceiling with all kinds of brass and iron pots and utensils hanging from it. There was an enormous black stove and a big butcher-block table with an elaborate mosaic surface.

A TV was embedded among the tiles on one wall. It was playing the news. There were pictures of New York City, enormous billboards, video screens the size of houses, lights flashing even in the daytime. I recognized the streets around Times Square.

'People are already beginning to gather for the big celebration tonight . . .' the newsreader said over the pictures.

Rose and Mike weren't here, but Dodger Jim and Milton One sat at the butcher-block table. They were eating rolls and eggs. Both had their eyes on the television when I walked in. Milton One was the first to turn to me. He lifted a roll.

'Good,' he said, his voice friendly and calm as always. 'You're in time for breakfast.'

'Where's Mike?' I asked him.

'Have some eggs, too,' said Dodger Jim, scraping some on to a plate for me.

'Where's Rose?' I said.

'Eat, Charlie,' said Dodger Jim. 'You're going to need it, believe me.'

'Organizers estimate there could be over three million people tonight in Times Square alone,' said the newsreader on the television.

I stared at the set, the pictures of smiling, laughing people bundled up for winter on the streets of New York. Snatches of conversation from the night before flashed in my sleep-fogged brain.

The whole point about Cylon Orange is its density. Six canisters is enough to wipe out four city blocks.

Four city blocks in New York City on New Year's Eve . . .

Could be a million people there. A million, at least.

I turned to Milton One, now calmly holding out a plate with eggs and bread on it.

A million people, at least.

'Where are they?' I said again. 'Rose and Mike. Where are they?'

'Mike is in the gym, studying maps,' said Milton One. 'Same as he's been doing most of the night. Rose is upstairs in the big room, calling everyone he knows, trying to convince them the threat is real. Same as he's been doing all night.'

'Patel's outside getting the plane ready,' Dodger Jim added.

'The plane . . . ?'

'Eat, Charlie. I mean it,' said Milton One. 'It's going to be a long day. You won't make it without food.'

'It's New Year's Eve,' I said desperately. I pointed at the television. 'They're already gathering in Times Square. We have to do something.'

'We will,' said Milton One in that same calm voice. 'And the first thing we're going to do is eat.'

I was frustrated but I saw the sense of it. I grabbed the plate. Grabbed some silverware off the butcher block. Quickly, I shoveled eggs into my mouth, swallowing them without tasting them.

'Tell me what happened last night,' I said through a mouthful of food. 'What did I see? What did I do?'

'You screamed like a banshee, for one thing,' said Dodger Jim. He smirked as he said it. I had given him a couple of knocks a while back during a fight we had. He didn't seem too sorry that I had been in pain.

Milton One rolled his eyes. 'The important thing you did is you remembered.'

The images began to clear. It came back to me. I stopped eating. 'The laptop. The laptop in the barracks.'

'Prince was apparently showing his friends the route he would take to get to Times Square. You saw a map,' said Milton One. 'A map of the New York City subway system with a route through the tunnels illuminated on it.'

'The subways . . .' I murmured.

'You were able to trace the route on a map Mike showed you.'

'Yes . . .' I said. It came back to me. 'That's right.'

'Security is extra tight,' said the newsreader on television, 'but, if people are afraid, they're not showing it. They're coming to the Big Apple in droves . . .'

On the screen, groups of people cheered and waved, celebrating the new year.

'Well, then, if we know where Prince is going . . .' I began to say.

But now Rose walked in. I – and Jim and Milton – turned to look at him.

He was wearing slacks and a wrinkled button-down shirt. He was carrying a battered leather briefcase in one hand. I would say he looked grim but he always looked grim – his mouth tight, his intelligent eyes alert. He looked at our expectant expressions. We didn't even have to ask the question out loud.

'I've got some assurances from the NYPD that there'll be a powerful police presence along the route we think Prince will take,' he told us with a sigh.

Slowly, I laid my empty plate down on the butcher-block table. 'A powerful police presence . . . ?' I said. 'What does that even mean?'

'Probably?' said Rose. 'It probably means it'll be harder for us to get where we're going.'

'Where are we going?' I said.

Before Rose could answer, I heard the Cessna engine start up outside. It roared and throbbed.

The next moment, Mike walked into the kitchen.

He nodded once at Rose. 'I've got the layout down solid,' he said. 'I know every inch of the way.'

Rose nodded back. 'Good.'

The detective set the leather briefcase on the butcher-block table. He opened it and reached in. He brought out a deadly-looking pistol, a 9mm Glock. It was already stuck in a shoulder holster. He handed the gun and holster to Mike. Mike was wearing a dark tracksuit. He pulled the jacket off and slipped the holster on over his sweatshirt. As he did, Rose brought another pistol out of the briefcase. This one he handed to me.

'Waterman gave you some weapons training, didn't he?' he asked.

'Some. The Homelanders gave me some too.'

'Good. I don't want you to blow your own head off.'

'I'll do my best.'

I took off the baseball jacket and strapped the weapon on over my sweatshirt. It felt heavy and somehow dark beneath my arm.

Now Patel appeared in the doorway. We could still hear the plane's engine rumbling and pulsing outside.

'We're ready to go,' said Patel.

I looked at them – all of them: Mike, Rose, Patel, Dodger Jim, Milton One. I looked from one face to another.

'What are we going to do?' I asked them.

For a moment, none of them answered. Then, finally, Mike said, 'We're going to stop them, Charlie.'

I stared at him. 'What do you mean?' I asked. 'Just us?'

Mike took a long breath. Then he nodded. 'We're all there is,' he said.

Chapter Twenty-seven

Dead in the Air

The Cessna flew low over green rolling hills. Then, after a while, Patel found the highway and we followed its winding white path. As the winter sun sank and the pale blue of the sky grew deeper, small cities appeared sparkling below us and then melded into thick forests or faded into empty fields.

Soon, more highways seemed to join the one we were following, becoming a snaky tangle of pavement amidst the surrounding foliage. More cities seemed to rise beneath us. In the intervals between them, we saw broad highways flanked with gas stations and malls. The dusk gathered slowly and the world turned gray.

I was sitting up front in the passenger seat again, with Rose behind me, Patel next to me, and Mike behind him. I peered through the side window at the changing light outside and the changing scene below.

'There's the river,' Patel said to me finally. His voice crackled over the headset and under the thrum of the engine.

I followed the gesture of his hand, looked ahead through the windshield and saw where the graying landscape reached what at first seemed like a sudden ending. Then the darker gray of the river became visible – a long, thick line. In a little while I could make out the water, the low December sun behind us sending a fanning, sparkling line across it to the far side.

'And look there,' said Patel, pointing to my side.

I turned and looked. Far off against the deep blue distance, I could make out the Manhattan skyline: a jagged dance of stone. The lights were just beginning to come on in some of the windows.

'Nice, huh?' said Patel kind of wistfully.

'Awesome,' I said. It was. An awesome, amazing city.

'I grew up there,' he went on. 'In Brooklyn, over on the other side.'

'No kidding.'

'I miss it now, I'll tell you.'

'Sure,' I said. 'Home, right?'

'Exactly. Home.'

'I miss mine, too,' I said – and I felt it. As far away as I'd been, as much trouble as I'd seen, I'd never felt as far from being reunited with my family and friends as I felt just then. Just then, to be honest, it seemed impossible that it would ever happen.

'A city like New York . . .' said Patel. I glanced over at him. He kept one hand resting lightly on the plane's yoke and the other lying limp on his leg – the way pilots do to keep from over-steering. He gave me a smile, trying to appear relaxed and cool. But I could tell he was feeling the pressure too. We all were. 'A city like New York gets into your blood somehow.'

'Does it?' I said doubtfully.

'You don't like it?'

'New York?' I shrugged. 'I like it OK.'

'You're more of a small-town guy, huh?'

'Yeah, I guess. To me, New York is kind of noisy and crowded and – I don't know – like, overwhelming.'

I heard Patel laugh a little over the headset. It was a sort of sad sound. He was thinking about home. 'I've heard people say that,' he said. 'I never noticed.'

'In New York, everyone's always walking around really fast with these serious looks on their faces. What's that about?'

He laughed again, fondly now. 'Everyone thinks he's very important and has something very important to do. That's what makes it New York.'

I nodded, smiling, but I wasn't thinking about New York. I was thinking about Spring Hill, my hometown. I remembered those quick flashing scenes I'd seen last night in the falling panic of my memory attack: scenes of my life back home, of being a kid. My mom driving me to the mall for my karate lessons; the baseball field in Oak Street Park where I played with Alex when we were still good friends; the path by the river where I walked with Beth when we were just getting to know one another . . . No one rushing around very much or looking very serious or feeling very important. A different kind of place.

'I guess it's all about what you're used to,' I said.

'I guess so,' said Patel.

We had reached the river now. Patel banked the plane to the right and started flying over the water, following its flow. The lowering sun sent its pale light pouring in through my window. I could feel the warmth of it on the side of my face. I looked ahead, watching the city skyline growing larger and larger, more and more lights coming on in the windows. Below us, too, and to the left, city streets sprung up on the river bank, stores and apartment towers, their lights also coming on. To the right, great surging brown cliffs sprung up darkly beside the water. As we flew toward the city, another small plane came toward us, flying just above us and to the left. It passed overhead, not far away at all.

'Almost there,' Patel said after a while. And then – as if he'd been thinking about it all this time – he said, 'To me, no matter where I go, New York is always home. When I'm away from sidewalks and tall buildings, I feel like I'm nowhere.'

I smiled, but it was hard for me to imagine feeling that way about such a big city. I had been on the run so long, been trying so hard to get back to my old life, that it felt to me like no one could want to be anywhere besides Spring Hill.

'For the last three years, I've had to live in Virginia for my job,' Patel went on. 'It just about drives me crazy. As soon as I can, I'm planning to bring my wife—'

My wife . . .

Those were the last words Patel ever spoke in this world. The next instant, the plane's side window shattered. The windshield went scarlet with Patel's blood and he was dead.

I could only sit there staring as he fell toward me, held in place by his shoulder-strap seat belt, his right hand still convulsively gripping the yoke.

I heard Rose roar out something in my ear. Dazed and horrified, I had only one second to look up and see the chopper that had pulled up alongside us in the darkening sky. A gunman sat balanced in its open door, his automatic rifle trained at our cockpit.

Milton One's words came back to me:

Prince will know you escaped. You're the one person who might know enough to catch up with him, so, even though he hasn't got a lot of manpower left, he's sure to be looking out for you, waiting for a chance to send someone after you.

The Homelanders had found us. They were here.

The wind rushed in through Patel's broken window.

Then, the next moment, Patel's body fell forward in his harness, pushing the yoke in. The plane pitched down.

We plunged, engine screaming, toward the river below.

Chapter Twenty-eight

Dogfight

There was nothing but noise and motion then, the seconds telescoping together into one endless instant of panic and terror. The roar of the plane's engine became a shriek. Beneath that shriek, I could hear both Rose and Mike shouting in my ear. The wind through the shattered window battered me as the airplane streaked downward like a meteor. With every endless instant, the river loomed larger and larger in the windshield. I had once read somewhere that hitting water hard from a great height was the same as hitting concrete. That was the thought – the one thought – that was flashing like a warning beacon in my mind.

I was moving before I thought to move. Grabbing Patel's limp, bloody body and pushing him back, I pried his hand off the pilot's yoke. I forced myself upright in my own seat as the plane started to turn into a sickening spiral. I had read a lot about planes while dreaming about being in the Air Force. I'd even read about how to pull one out of spins and dives. It was tricky stuff. You had to get it right or you could lose control completely and drop helplessly out of the sky like a stone.

But there was no choice. I had to do something, try something.

I grabbed the yoke in front of me. A hundred different ideas flashed through my head, all of them jumbled together with the screaming engine and the confused, jumbled shouts in my headset from Mike and Rose. There was nothing in the windshield now but water, closer and closer with every instant we dived.

I acted on instinct. I pulled the throttle back, bringing the engine to idle so that it wasn't thrusting us toward the earth. I rolled the wings over level. Patel's corpse shifted and fell toward me. I had to reach out with one hand and push him away again.

Now I drew up on the stick. It took some muscle to lift the heavy nose of the plane. The Cessna lost speed rapidly as it lifted, the river sinking out of the windshield, the dark blue of the sky and the lighted city skyline reappearing.

Only at the last second did it occur to me that if we lost any more speed the wings would stall and we would drop again. We were now only a couple of hundred feet off the earth. If the wings stalled at this point, we would never be able to recover in time.

I leveled the plane, hit the throttle and gunned the engine back to full. The engine started its stuttering roar again. The plane seemed to hover in the air a second as if deciding whether or not to fall.

Then the engine's power took hold and pushed the plane forward. The Cessna steadied and began to climb away from the river. I started breathing again. I'd done it. I'd pulled us out of the dive.

My headset filled with the sound of Mike and Rose cheering and shouting my name. The nose of the plane lifted, pointing up toward the sky. I felt a thrill of achievement and relief.

Then the chopper – and the gunman – pulled up alongside us again.

I caught sight of the helicopter in the corner of my eye. I looked over – the wind through the broken window whipping my face. I saw the small two-seater whirlybird hovering beside us, the gunman sitting in the open door. I saw him lift his automatic rifle once again. This time, it was pointing directly at me.

In pure, wild fear, I turned the yoke in my hand, hit the rudder with my foot. The Cessna gave a loud groaning buzz and swung to the right, away from the chopper. Over that noise and the shouts from Mike and Rose, I heard no gunshots. But I saw a spark fly off the plane's nose cone and I knew we were under fire. My stomach rolled as I pushed the plane into a sharp circle.

'Here he comes again, Charlie!' Mike shouted.

I looked around but, for a long, long moment as the plane turned, I could not find the chopper. Then I saw it again as we came around. The whirling machine had lifted up above me. The shooter was trying to reposition himself in the doorway so he could fire down at us. I had to get away from him – fast – now.

There was no time to think – and that was a good thing. Because, if I'd had time to think, I'd have realized we had no chance of survival. I had only the most basic flying skills. I could guide a plane in flight – which is pretty easy if you don't have to do anything too fancy. And I could land – at least I had landed a few times when I had an instructor sitting in the seat beside me telling me what to do. But to take evasive action – to outmaneuver an expert pilot in a chopper – to stay away from a hail of automatic-weapon bullets while keeping out of a stall – that was way beyond me. There was no chance I could pull it off.

That's what I would have thought if I'd had time to think, so, like I say, it was a good thing there was no time. I simply turned the plane again and pushed its nose down, diving right beneath the chopper before the gunman could get off another shot.

I heard Rose let out something between a curse and a prayer, his usually flat voice rising with fear as we continued diving across the river. But I couldn't level out. I couldn't see the helicopter behind me but I knew it must be turning around, repositioning itself for an attack. I had to keep turning, twisting, diving, dodging.

Up ahead, I saw high-rise brick buildings – apartments in one of the towns or boroughs outside Manhattan – I didn't know which one. I pointed the plane straight at the rising brick walls.

Once again, my headset filled up with shouts from Mike and Rose.

'Charlie, watch out!'

'Pull up, Charlie! We're gonna hit!'

But I didn't pull up. I forced the plane to sweep down out of the sky, knowing all the while that the chopper was right behind me.

I came off the river low, flying right over the street, right down the corridor formed by the brick towers on either side. We had lost so much altitude that, when I glanced to the side, I saw the brownstone rooftops right next to me. I saw the upper windows in the buildings to my right and left. I could even see some shocked faces staring out at us through the glass.

I strained against my seat belt as I tried to look around, tried to spot the chopper, find out where it was. It was nowhere in sight.

I heard a scream – two screams.

Mike: 'Watch out!'

Then Rose: 'Charlie!'

I looked ahead – and let out a scream of my own.

A railway bridge was suddenly there, right in front of me. We were soaring right at it. I could already read the graffiti painted on its side.

I was about to pull up on the yoke so we could rise above it. But just then, the chopper appeared, above and in front of me. It was blocking my escape route. If the plane lifted up now, we'd crash right into the chopper.

The Cessna barreled through the sky toward the side of the bridge. The chopper hovered above, turning so that the gunman could take his shot. To my left and right, the way was blocked by the brick towers.

My mind went blank. I couldn't think of a way out. My head was filled with the sound of Mike and Rose shouting in my ear.

Then I saw the intersection, just before the bridge. I banked the plane and we went roaring around the corner and down the cross street.

The Cessna went over almost on to its side as we made the turn. The engine noise filled my ears, a howl like a baby's. The sickening swirling scene in the windshield was like something out of a video game – one of those sequences where you have to dodge through obstacles – as the plane slipped through the gap between one brick tower and another. Of course, in video games, you have an endless number of lives. In reality, you only have one. It makes a big difference in how you play.

For an instant, I caught glimpses of people on the street below. We were actually so near the ground I could make out the horrified looks on their faces as they stood with their mouths open, gaping up at us.

Then, with a panicky jerk at the yoke, I leveled the Cessna out before it could come full around and smash into one of the buildings. The plane straightened and wobbled down the center of the street. I gave it gas and lifted the nose. We rose and rose until we were above the tower rooftops.

For a moment, I had a feeling of freedom, of escape, a sense that we were pulling away, speeding for the open sky.

Then the gunman struck again.

This time, I not only couldn't hear the shots, I didn't see the chopper or the shooter at all. But I felt this terrifying, stuttering jolt as the bullets ripped into the fuselage. For a second, I felt the plane was flying out of control. Then the yoke seemed to grip. I lowered the nose and dove toward the street again, turning at the same time to avoid another round of bullets.

I caught sight of the chopper as it heeled to one side to come chasing down after me. Then I looked out ahead. We were diving down toward a street of smaller buildings: low, old, brick-and-wood shops and houses. Old wooden telephone poles lined the streets.

The pavement rushed up toward us. I leveled the plane out, close to the ground, and we shot ahead. A moment later, sparks flew from the plane's left wing and I knew the helicopter had come down after us, that the gunman was firing at us from behind.

Desperate – terrified out of my skull, to put it plainly – I stared ahead, steering down the middle of the street. I saw people running for cover, cars screeching to the curb, drivers jumping out and dashing into stores and doorways. The road now lay clear in front of me. The dusk was settling over it – a blue-gray darkness overcoming the last light of day.

I had an idea. I guess you could call it an idea. Moving that fast, that low, that close to buildings and the street, with the chopper on my tail and the gunman taking shots at me, I wasn't exactly thinking, not in a way you'd call thinking, anyway. But things flashed into my mind – half thoughts, half images, half formed. There was no time to sort them out or make decisions about them. But there was also no choice but to act – and pray.

What came to me was the idea of telephone lines: the telephone wires that go from pole to pole. It came to me that telephone wires were deadly to low-flying planes. You couldn't see them until the last minute – in this light you probably couldn't see them at all – and, if you ran into them, they grabbed you, tangled you up and tossed you to the ground.

As our plane shot down the street toward the corner, I realized there must be wires right in front of me, crossing the street from one set of poles to another. In seconds, we would hit them and go down.

So here was my idea – my crazy sort of idea. I let the plane sink lower. Lower. So low that the windows of three-story houses flashed by me. We were seconds away from reaching the corner – and we were headed directly at the wires, the telephone wires invisible in the twilight.

I waited. Waited.

Then I started to lift the Cessna's nose. Not fast at first, not hard, just enough to make the plane rise a bit. I sent up a prayer that I'd have time to get enough altitude to go over the phone lines. I prayed the wires wouldn't snag the landing gear that hung down from the bottom of the fuselage. I prayed – and lifted the nose further.

We rose and rose . . . And then there they were. I saw them: the phone wires crossing the street, parallel black lines like the lines on a sheet of music. I pulled back hard on the yoke and gave the plane full throttle. We lifted up and up suddenly. The wires passed underneath us. And then I banked the plane hard to the left.

The plane came around fast, low over the low rooftops. We made a quick semi-circle and were just in time to see what happened next.

As I'd guessed, the chopper was right behind us. It had come down low to trail us, to try and get another shot. It had been right on our tail, the gunman taking aim.

But the pilot hadn't thought about the wires.

As the Cessna turned, I looked out the window and saw the chopper start its rise to come after us. It never made it. Instead, it seemed to stop stark still – just stop right there in the air above the street as if it had been caught in the hand of an invisible giant. It had flown right into the phone wires. The next second, the force of the impact flipped it upside down, just like that.

The gunman was hurled off his perch in the open doorway. With the Cessna still turning, still rising, I saw his black form tumbling through the air toward the empty street. His body smacked against the pavement so hard I could almost feel the thud.

Then the chopper came down right on top of him.

The whirlybird smacked into the asphalt and blew. The explosion sent a billowing dome of red flame up into the air.

The thunder of the blast reached me even over my headset, even over the throb of the engine. The blast shook the Cessna as it climbed up out of its turn.

Mike and Rose stopped shouting in my headset. We were all silent. I faced forward. The flicker of flame played over the windshield as we climbed toward the darkening sky. I kept turning until I spotted the river, in the distance now. I headed for the water, the nose up, the plane gaining altitude, the city buildings sinking away below me.

I breathed a sigh of relief.

Then I smelled the smoke.

A second later, a black cloud lifted up from the fuselage. It was quickly blown apart by the wash of air from the propeller.

'Fire!' Mike shouted.

And then Rose shouted: 'We're on fire!'

I turned to look across Patel's slack body, out through the window. I saw a lick of flame rising to the shattered pane.

My relief vanished in a nauseating swirl of fresh fear. Any second, I knew, the fire would reach the fuel lines. They would ignite, and the flames would rush to the gas tanks in the wings.

Then the plane would explode like a bomb.

Chapter Twenty-nine

Crash

Cut the engine!

At this point, I didn't know whether Mike or Rose shouted the words into my headset, or whether the words just shouted themselves into my mind. But I knew that's what I had to do: cut the engine – stop the fuel from running through the lines before the fire reached them.

I pulled the throttle all the way back. I pulled the red knob – the choke. The engine sputtered once and died. The plane went bizarrely quiet, just hanging in air – no engine, no power. Another second and the nose pitched down toward the city below. The black smoke billowed up. The smell in the cockpit grew thicker.

We were going down. There was no way out of it. I couldn't turn the engine back on, couldn't start the gas flowing, not with the plane in flames. I could glide for a while, but we'd keep sinking. Eventually, we were going to crash land.

That is, if we didn't explode first.

I looked out through the windshield, scanning the scene in

front of me, looking for a place where I could make a safe landing. The river was too far. We'd go smashing into the streets before we got there. I might try to land on the highway, but I could see in the gathering dark that it was thick with headlights, thick with cars, everyone heading toward Manhattan for the New Year's Eve celebration.

Lifting my eyes then, I spotted a deeper darkness in the distance to my left. Hard to tell from where I was, but I thought it might be a park. There was a chance, anyway. The only chance, as far as I could see.

I turned the yoke and the plane banked toward that deeper darkness.

With the engine off, the power gone, the plane continued to sink steadily downward in a slow forward glide. I tried to keep the nose pointed at just the right angle, just low enough to keep our speed up so the wings wouldn't stall, but high enough to keep us aloft until we reached the open space of the park. If it was a park. If there was open space.

Mike and Rose had fallen silent again. And I was silent. The plane was quiet except for the wind coming in through the shattered window. I felt a knot of tension in my stomach as I waited to see whether there'd be anyplace to land.

As if that weren't bad enough, suddenly, I heard a throbbing noise to my left. I felt my heart seize in my chest as another chopper appeared in the sky beside me. It took me a moment before I saw that it was the police. And now there were two choppers – no, three. Alerted to the action in the sky and the crash of the Homelanders' whirlybird, the cops were coming after us.

There was nothing I could do about it now. I had to give my full attention to the plane.

My pulse was beating hard in my head. My mouth was dry. My hand felt unsteady on the controls.

Mike leaned forward from the back seat. He clapped his hand on my shoulder. I stole a look at him – catching a look at Patel, too, where he hung forward in his harness, dead. Mike also looked at Patel, then we looked at one another.

'That was some pretty fancy flying you did back there, chucklehead,' Mike said into his headset mic. His voice came over my set.

'Flying is one thing,' I told him. 'Landing's a lot tougher.'

'Stay cool, pal. You can do this.'

I nodded and faced forward. The plane sank lower. It *was* a park up ahead – I could see it now. I could make out the bare branches of the winter trees. There was a cluster of them – then open space beyond: a long field of grass. If I could stay high enough to clear the treetops, I'd have a shot at landing there. It wouldn't be easy, though. Especially with my muscles so tight with fear I could barely move.

'You've landed planes before, right?' said Rose nervously.

'Absolutely,' I said. *At airports*, I thought. With big, long, flat runways. And an instructor in the seat beside me telling me what to do. And a plane with a working engine so I could pull and go around and try again if I made a mistake. It was a little different being alone like this, heading for a park in deep twilight, with no engine, with only one chance to get it right. And, oh yeah, did I mention the plane was on fire?

'You're gonna do fine,' said Mike, as if he'd read my mind.

I was glad he had so much faith in me. That made one of us.

The Cessna dipped down lower and lower. At that slow speed, every breath of wind made the plane jump and wobble. The controls felt unsteady in my hand.

It was getting pretty dark down there below but I could still see the trees plainly and the field beyond them was becoming clearer as we came closer. I could sense the police choppers hovering around me, but I didn't dare to look. I was too busy, peering down too hard, trying too desperately to make sure there were no people in the park below who would get in my way. If there were, it would be a disaster. But – no – the park seemed to have emptied out as the cold winter night came on.

I started, held my breath, as I caught a glimpse of flame in the window beside me. By the time I looked over, it was gone. But I could still smell the smoke. I knew the fire was growing. I knew that time was running out.

The darkness seemed to close over us as we glided down and down toward the level of the trees. As the plane got closer to the field, I could see the ground was less flat than it had looked from further away. I could see the uneven contours, the slight rises – and the obstacles, too – trash cans, benches, sand boxes. It was hard to find enough room to set the plane down safely.

But I was out of options. There was no way to climb back toward the sky, that was for sure. The plane went on sinking steadily. My heart banged in my chest. The Lord's Prayer played in my head like a broken record. The tops of the trees rose toward me.

Then everything seemed to speed up. The end came very quickly.

We went over the trees – close, very close, but we cleared them. Now the dark ground rose up suddenly like a beast's back. I lowered the plane's flaps and lifted the nose. The plane dropped fast, rushing forward at the same time. The field came up to meet us, the park racing past the windows.

A hovering moment – then the wheels touched down – hard – very hard. The jolt threw me forward against the harness and brought my teeth snapping together. The plane bounced and lifted back into the air and dropped down again even harder this time. I tried to control the Cessna with the foot pedals, but the nose skewed further and further to the side.

Then the plane turned and dipped. There was a sickening crunch. The landing gear seemed to collapse under us and the wing thumped against the earth. There was a loud crash as something smacked into the rear of the fuselage. The plane went slantwise.

Then we stopped. It was over. We were down.

Everything was quiet. I sat there, dazed.

Then Mike started shouting. 'Get out, Charlie! Get out! Get out fast – now – before it blows!'

His voice brought me back to myself. Quickly, I ripped off my harness. I found the door latch in the dark and shoved the door open. I tumbled out into the cold December air.

Confusion. The plane on fire. The Cessna's crumpled silhouette flickering into relief as the flames rose. The police choppers hovered above me, sending white spotlights down on top of me. I couldn't hear their engines. I couldn't hear anything but my own heart pounding in my ears.

Then I ripped my headset off and I heard the pound of the choppers and I heard Mike shouting.

'Come on, come on!'

I saw him inside the plane. He was struggling to get out of the back seat before the Cessna exploded. There were no doors in the back. He and Rose had to push the seat forward and climb over it before they could exit.

'Mike!' I shouted.

I rushed toward the burning Cessna. Avoiding the rising flames, I stuck my head in through the open passenger door. Mike was in the back, struggling with Rose.

'I can't . . .' I heard Rose say. 'My leg. Go on, Mike, get out.'

I saw Mike trying to shove him into the front seat.

I pulled the front seat forward to make way for him. I felt heat as the fire rose beneath me. The police spotlights swept over me, then were gone and in the sudden dark I saw the flickering red light of the flames.

'Clear out, Charlie!' Mike shouted. 'She's gonna go! Clear out!'

I ignored him. There was no way, no way I was going to leave them there. I reached deeper into the smothering smoke and heat and grabbed hold of Rose. I tried to drag him forward into the front seat. He let out a shout of pain.

'My leg!'

'Lift him toward me, Mike!' I shouted.

'Get out, I said!' he shouted back.

'Lift him to me or we all die!'

Mike let out a curse at my stubbornness but did what I said and hoisted Rose up until I could grab him under the arms. Rose let out a scream of pain as I dragged him into the front seat. He went on screaming and I went on pulling him until we were both outside, both clear of the fire.

I lost my balance and tumbled backwards on to the grass. Rose fell on top of me. He screamed one more time and rolled off me. I sat up as the police spotlight swept across us. Then it was gone and there was just the red firelight, bright and steady now. The flames rose up from under the fuselage, up over the cockpit, blocking the exit.

'Mike!' I screamed.

I scrambled to my feet.

'No!' Rose shouted at me. 'Stay back!'

I rushed toward the plane. I felt the heat of the fire tighten the skin on my face. I fought my way toward it, trying to beat the smoke and flames away with my hands.

'Mike! Mike!' I kept screaming.

And Rose was screaming behind me, 'West, get back! Get back!'

The noise of the low-flying choppers filled the air. Their spotlights swept the darkness. The shadows of tree branches moved crazily everywhere like skeletons in a dance. There was the noise of sirens, too, growing louder. Cop cars approaching in the night.

Through all the confusion, another sound reached me. A sort of hollow bump. Was that it? Was the plane about to explode? The flames rose up higher around me.

The next second, something hit me hard in the chest. I went flying backwards, away from the plane, backwards out of the firelight, out of the spotlights, into the night.

I went down on my back hard – and Mike came down hard on top of me. He had thrown himself out of the plane, through the flames. He'd thrown himself right into me, tackled me, driving me to the earth.

Just in time. The Cessna exploded.

There was no big blast, just a dull, hollow, echoless thud. The flames expanded upward and outward in a spreading ball. The three police helicopters, flying low, shot up, away into the air to escape the fire. Their spotlights yawed and criss-crossed.

Chunks of hot metal and drifting fire started to come down all around me. I tried to dodge them but Mike held me where I was, covering my body with his.

When he rose up, I saw him clearly in the firelight, his face streaked with dirt, the dancing flames reflected in his eyes.

'You all right?' he said.

I rolled over and sat up, feeling the heat from the fire wash over me.

'Patel,' I said. 'He's still in there.'

'No, he's not,' said Mike. 'It's just his body, Charlie. Patel is gone.'

I didn't like to think of Patel's body stuck in that burning plane, but Mike was right, and there was nothing I could do about it now.

'What about you?' Mike said again. 'Are you hurt?'

'No,' I said. 'Not much. I'm all right.'

'Rose?' said Mike.

I turned and saw Rose sitting up halfway, clutching at his leg with one hand. His face was contorted with pain.

'I'll be OK,' he said through gritted teeth. 'But my leg's busted.'

'All right,' said Mike. 'We'll get you help.'

'No,' said Rose. He had to shout now over the roar of the flames and the growing howl of the sirens and the beat choppers, too, which hung higher in the air to stay clear of the fire, but were still directly above us. 'You've got to get out of here – before the cops arrive. If the police stop us, we'll never get there in time.'

Lit by the flames from the plane, Mike scanned the area. I could see him thinking it through.

'Go,' said Rose. 'I'll be all right. I'll get them to help, send reinforcements. They have to believe me now. All those lives at stake . . . They have to. Go, Mike. Go on.'

After another second, Mike nodded once. He turned to me.

'Let's do it,' he said.

He didn't have to say it twice. I leapt to my feet.

Without another word, Mike took off, sprinting away from the spotlights into the deeper shadows beneath the trees.

I paused. I nodded once at Rose – one nod of goodbye and thanks. Rose nodded back.

Then I followed Mike into the darkness.

Chapter Thirty

Escape

I had no idea where we were or where we were going. I just followed Mike. He seemed to know the way, dodging and weaving through the park with absolute certainty. I remembered Milton One had told me he'd been studying maps all night.

At first, the choppers didn't come after us. I think they'd lost sight of us, trying to get away from the exploding plane. But, as Mike and I raced through the darkness, I heard the pulsing throb of their rotors growing louder behind us. I looked over my shoulder and saw their powerful spotlights sweeping the night. One of them seemed to have stayed behind with Rose. The other two were looking for us.

'Keep close,' Mike shouted back to me.

I did. He ran along a line of trees, his path tracing the shapes of their shadows. The shifting patches of dark thrown by the tree trunks and the bare branches gave us some cover and Mike made the most of it. All around us, the chopper spotlights swept back and forth over the grass, searching and searching.

But they'd lost us. By the time we reached the edge of the park, the throb of the rotors was growing dimmer as the choppers headed off over the trees in the wrong direction.

Following Mike, I stepped off the soft grass on to hard pavement. And I stopped. Mike was there, standing at the edge of the sidewalk. I followed his gaze, looked up and saw tall buildings standing black against the night. Their windows were broken and lightless. They seemed abandoned.

Mike slapped my shoulder and gestured with his head. He started running again. I went after him.

We wove down these dark, abandoned streets. There were no people anywhere. It seemed the city – or the borough – wherever we were – was completely empty.

Then we turned a corner – and, suddenly, there were the people. On a broad, brightly lit boulevard, a large crowd moved in a steady line past stores and under streetlamps. There were police everywhere too, standing on the outskirts of the crowd, scanning the people closely as they passed.

Mike and I stood on the corner of a shadowy side street. He swiped at his face with his hands, trying to use his own sweat to wash the grime off his cheeks, trying to make himself look as normal as possible. I did the same.

When he was done, Mike gave a quick tug at my elbow and started moving again. I followed him.

We joined the masses, moving with the human tide. In the distance, I could hear sirens, lots of sirens. Then there came the beat of the choppers, too. I looked up and saw a police helicopter hovering in the air right above us. When I glanced over at the patrolmen on the ground, they were all murmuring into their walkie-talkies. I figured they were getting the word about the crash in the park and our escape. I figured they were being told to look out for us. I felt the policemen's eyes on me as we passed by them – I felt sure they were all looking straight at me. But I guess Mike knew that, in a crowd like that, it would be hard to pick out any one person. Anyway, he shoved his way into the center of the throng and I went with him and no one spotted us.

We walked steadily along, pushed and carried by the flow of people. After a few minutes, I saw where we were heading. There was a subway stop on the corner up ahead. It was a stairway leading down into the sidewalk, the opening in the pavement surrounded by a low green barrier. At least one branch of the river of people was flowing into the opening and cascading down the stairs. Another few seconds, and Mike and I were cascading down with them.

As the lights of the streets and the cold of the evening air gave way to the muted light and the dank stuffy atmosphere of the enclosed subway station, I felt myself relax a little. I felt safer here, below ground, out of the open, away from the choppers.

As we reached the bottom of the stairs, I looked around the station, peering over the heads of the people around me. There was a ticket booth in a tiled enclosure and ticket machines against the wall and a row of turnstiles leading to the subway platform. There were more cops also, patrolmen in blue uniforms: one in the ticket area and two more that I could see on the platform, watching the crowds.

Mike muscled his way to the ticket machines and came back to me with a ticket. Then he motioned me toward the turnstiles. The crowd grew denser as the turnstiles slowed the people's progress. We pushed in close to the thickening mass, reached the turnstiles, swiped our tickets and pushed through. We walked directly past one of the patrolmen guarding the platform. My shoulder nearly brushed him as I went by, we were that close. I felt my breath catch as his eyes went over me, but then we were past him and, the next moment, the train shot into the station, the windows flashing as it roared and rattled past.

The train slowed; stopped. The doors opened. No one left the car. The crowd just poured in like water into a funnel. I had to shoulder my way through the dense mass to make it on. Then the doors closed and Mike and I were crushed together, packed in so tightly with the others I could hardly breathe.

The train started moving again.

Someone shouted drunkenly, 'Happy New Year!'

We headed into Manhattan.

Chapter Thirty-one

Into the Darkness

It was a long ride. The train rushed through the tunnel, blackness at the windows. The crowd held me tight, immobile – which was just as well. Left to stand alone, I might have collapsed. I was that exhausted.

The madness of the past hours flashed through my mind. The flight over the river. The sudden death of Patel. The wild helicopter chase close to the city streets. The sight of the chopper caught in the phone wires. The gunman falling through the air to his death. The chopper exploding. And the Cessna, landing without power in the park. The crash. The fire. Getting Rose and Mike out. The race through the streets . . .

And New Year's Eve was just beginning.

It was not so long ago, I was an ordinary guy, I thought, an ordinary kid in an ordinary town, doing the sorts of things you do every day. You know: getting through school, hanging with your friends, thinking about girls and sports and computers and did I mention girls? There were days in that old life when I wondered if anything really exciting would ever happen to me. There were days now – lots of days – when I wondered if the excitement would ever stop, if I would ever have a quiet dinner with Beth or play a round of *Medal of Honor* with my gang, or just, I don't know, listen to music, shoot some hoops, whatever, you know, the things you do.

I missed life. I missed ordinary life. I wondered if I would ever see ordinary life again. I didn't realize how good a thing it was until I lost it.

I stood crushed in the crowd. I stared into empty space. I guess I was feeling sorry for myself a little. Sorry and so tired I didn't know how I was going to make it through.

The train crossed into Manhattan and headed south. I stared into space. Something funny came into my mind then: English class. I know: what a weird thing to think about. But suddenly I saw myself sitting there at my desk, listening to upbeat, roly-poly Mrs Smith reading a Rudyard Kipling poem at the front of the class.

'If you can force your heart and nerve and sinew/To serve your turn long after they are gone,/And so hold on when there is nothing in you/Except the Will which says to them: "Hold on!" '

It was strange, I thought. At the time she read the poem, I don't think I was even listening that closely. But now the words came back as if they had been written specifically for me: *Hold on when there is nothing in you except the Will which says to them . . .*

'Hold on,' said Mike, his voice rising above the roar and rattle of the car. 'It's the next stop.'

I saw the train begin to slow. Lights flashed in the darkness of the window. Then the scene out there opened up into a large station: Columbus Circle. The train stopped. The door opened. It was like releasing water through a dam. The people poured out with enormous force. Even if I'd wanted to stay on the train, I wouldn't have been able to. I was carried out on to the platform in the tide.

I wasn't prepared for what I saw. The crowds had been dense out in the borough, but they were nothing compared to this.

The station was big – a broad interior space with several platforms, several tracks, visible through columns. People seemed to be coming from every direction, pouring up stairways and out of corridors, converging in front of the exits. More people than I'd ever seen in my life.

The massive tide flowed toward the rows and rows of stairs up toward the exit. At first, I was carried helplessly along, up the stairs, toward the turnstiles. But, before we could exit the station, Mike caught hold of my arm and pulled me to the side, against a massive swirling mosaic on the wall. We pressed against the multicolored tiles as the people flowed past us. Another, opposing tide of people was flowing back into the station, back down toward the platforms, at the same time.

Mike rose up on tiptoe, stretched his neck and looked around.

Then I heard him murmur, 'This way.'

We joined the flow of people moving away from the exits, down a different flight of stairs, back toward the platforms. I hardly knew where we were going. I just followed Mike, and went with the crowd.

We came on to another platform now. A train had just arrived here. Its doors stood open and people were pouring out, then pouring in. The people who had just left the train were moving in a sludgy mass toward the exit. Others, who couldn't fit on the train, were lining up along the edge of the platform to wait for the next one.

Mike kept moving, pushing against the thick cluster of bodies until we broke through and forced our way down the platform. I kept right behind Mike, but it wasn't easy. I had to shoulder my way through the small spaces in the crowd.

After a couple of minutes, the mob seemed to thin suddenly – the grip of the crowd relaxed around me. Now I saw where Mike was going.

The platform ended just up ahead. There was a metal railing and then, beyond it, the darkness of the train tunnels and the tracks. A single police officer stood guard there, his hands behind his back, his legs akimbo, his back erect, his eyes moving and alert.

As the crowd fell away behind us, Mike continued down the platform toward the patrolman. Mike's moustache curled as he broke into a rare, bright, toothy smile.

'Hey, Mike, where you going?' I murmured. I couldn't believe he was walking right toward the cop.

But Mike either didn't hear me or ignored me. He didn't answer. He didn't even look my way.

Now Mike was just about to reach the police officer.

Nervous, I turned and looked behind me. I scanned the packed platform to see if anyone was watching us. We had gone beyond the end of the train, beyond the clusters of people. Everyone was intent on where he was going. No one was paying any attention to us at all.

Then I faced forward – and stopped short. My mouth dropped open.

The policeman was gone. He had just vanished. I had turned away for only a second and when I turned back, he seemed to have simply gone up in smoke.

Only not. Because then I looked down and saw him. Good thing it was noisy in the station, because I actually gasped out loud.

The cop lay crumpled and unconscious on the concrete platform. Mike stood over him, beckoning to me urgently.

The next instant, in one smooth, silent movement, Mike vaulted over the low railing and dropped down on to the train tracks below. As I stood there in shock, he raced away into the darkness of the train tunnel.

There was no time to hesitate. No time to think. Besides, what choice did I have? I took two long steps and reached the fallen patrolman. He was already stirring, already moving his hand to his head as he regained consciousness.

I stepped past the patrolman quickly, grabbed the railing, and vaulted over.

Then I was running after Mike, along the train track, into the tunnel, into the dark beneath the city.

Chapter Thirty-two

Beneath the City

We ran into the tunnel, a close corridor with the train track laid tightly between the walls. We ran down the center of the track. There was nowhere else to go.

'Watch out for the rail,' Mike said to me over his shoulder.

'The what?'

'The rail.' He stopped so short I almost ran into him. He took me roughly by the shoulder and pointed. 'The third rail.'

I saw it. A rail with a protective covering running over the top of it.

'There's enough electricity going through that thing to blow your head off,' Mike said. 'Literally. Step on it and you're fried.'

I nodded, breathing hard. 'Good thing to know.'

'Come on.'

And we were off again. Running through the tunnel down the center of the track.

As we went, I glanced back over my shoulder. I saw the platform behind us. That is, I saw a tall rectangle of light where the tunnel ended and the platform began. Some of the crowd was visible. The patrolman was visible too. He was just sitting up, just reaching uncertainly for the railing to pull himself to his feet. I wondered what Mike had done to him, but I didn't ask. I knew he had a hundred techniques for knocking a guy out without hurting him.

The tracks turned gradually to the left. When I glanced back again, the platform was out of sight. Nothing but tunnel visible back there now; up ahead, nothing but Mike moving through the narrow darkness.

It seemed like we ran a long while in that suffocating close space before Mike stopped to catch his breath. I stopped beside him. I bent forward with my hands on my knees, panting, taking in great gasps of the dirty, gritty underground air. When I lifted my head, I could see, by the dim lights hung on the walls all around, that we had come to the end of the tunnel. We stood on the edge of a broader area. It was like some kind of vast underground vault or something. There were columns here and there and, between them, I could see other tracks running off in different directions. I could hear the trains moving in the distance, signal lights sizzling and track switches clicking. I could smell smoke and garbage and the filth of the place. I could see green lights in the distance turning red and red lights turning green. When I raised my eyes toward the ceiling, I could feel the city up there, the enormous city packed with people for New Year's Eve. I could imagine them gathering in great crowds, wearing costumes, setting off noise makers, celebrating, ready to party, completely unaware we were down here and that Prince was down here somewhere, waiting to set off his deadly chemical and kill as many of them as he could.

I lowered my eyes again – and gave a sort of jump. I saw rats snuffling along the iron rails, looking for something to eat. I made a face as I swallowed my disgust.

'Let's go, Mike,' I said. 'Which direction?'

A rat went near Mike's foot. He kicked it away. 'South,' he said. 'If we keep heading toward Times Square we should intersect with Prince's route at the 48th Street junction.' With that, he reached under his jacket and pulled out his 9mm. 'At least, I hope so,' he added. He checked the gun's safety and chambered a round.

I reached under my baseball jacket to the shoulder holster there. I drew out my own weapon. I did what he did: checked the safety, chambered a round. The gun felt heavy in my hands – heavy and deadly.

'We're gonna need these, pal,' Mike told me. 'Brace yourself.'

I nodded. 'I'll do what I have to do.'

He nodded back. 'I know you will.'

'I can't believe it's come down to just us,' I said. I could hear the anxiety in my own voice. I didn't much like the sound of it. 'Don't you think we'll get any help at all? The police? Homeland security? Anyone? They're just gonna let this happen?'

'I don't know,' said Mike. 'You can bet Rose is talking their ears off as we speak, trying to convince them that this is real.'

'With our luck, they'll probably arrest Rose while they leave Prince free to do his thing.'

He gave a laugh that wasn't much of a laugh at all. 'Could be.'

'We don't even know how many men Prince has. Seems a lot for just you and me to handle on our own.'

'Yes, it does.' He holstered his gun. 'You ready?'

I stuffed my weapon back under my jacket. 'Yeah.'

'Me too. Let's go.'

We took off. Instead of moving down the tracks now, we moved across them, from track to track, leaping whenever we had to cross the third rail. We moved through the big underground chamber. As my eyes traveled up along the columns and walls, I saw not only the dim lights here and there, but also security cameras. That made me nervous at first. Could the police see us down here? But then I noticed that every single camera we passed was busted and hung useless in its metal frame.

Mike stopped again, holding out his hand. I felt a breath of wind rush over me. I heard switches clicking through the great chamber.

'What?' I said.

'Train,' said Mike.

Then I saw it – a bright headlight appearing down one of the tunnels. The wind grew stronger as the train pushed the air in the tunnel toward us. The rattle of the cars grew louder.

The light grew bigger, brighter. Rats, feeling the rumble, came waddling quickly out of the tunnel. My gorge rose in my throat as I saw one humped rodent the size of a cat. Disgusting.

'This way,' said Mike.

He took off across the tracks, leaping over another third rail, then leaping again – over a rat this time. I followed him across one set of tracks, then another. Then, the train rushed out of its tunnel.

It was close – big – loud. I could feel the ground vibrating hard under my feet as it went by. I saw the lighted windows flashing past, the people crushed together inside.

Then the train was gone. Mike and I kept running, heading across the underground chamber.

Now we entered another tunnel. The walls closed in on either side of us again. The darkness closed in and the air got thick. I trained my eyes on the tunnel's end – an archway up ahead.

But before we were anywhere near it, I felt a breath of wind on the back of my neck. I felt a tremor under my feet.

I looked back over my shoulder.

'Mike . . .'

He looked back, too. There was a light behind us. The wind was getting stronger. Shadows of rats were rushing after us on the tracks.

A train. It had come into the tunnel. It was heading toward us. This time, there was no room to get out of its way.

'Go,' said Mike.

He ran at top speed and I ran right after. Fast as we could, we windmilled down the tracks toward the opening at the end of the tunnel.

The train came after us. The wind grew stronger at my back. The rumble grew louder. The ground seemed to buck around like a wild horse trying to hurl us out of the saddle.

I glanced back again. I thought my heart would just stop cold. The train's headlight was suddenly huge, bright, blinding. The train was bearing down on top of us. There was no way we would ever reach the end of the tunnel before it ran us down.

I faced forward and doubled my speed – and, even so, Mike stayed ahead of me. And the train got closer. The wind got stronger as the big engine pushed a wave of air before it. The tunnel filled with the oncoming roar. I could practically feel the front end of the train at my heels.

Mike glanced over his shoulder. I could see his mouth moving, his teeth bared, as he shouted something to me. But the words were washed away by the rush of wind and the rattle of the wheels.

Now Mike spun round, stopped, grabbed my arm. He pulled me toward the edge of the track. What good was that? There was no space between the train and the walls. If we tried to duck to the side, we'd be crushed.

But, in the spreading light from the train's headlight, I saw something low on the wall near the floor: a deeper darkness. Some kind of opening.

Mike dragged me toward it. The train was just seconds

away, barreling at us. The noise and light washed away every thought.

Mike disappeared into the opening in the wall, dragging me in after him. I had to stoop down to get my head in beneath the arch.

Then we were in. And just in time: the train hammered past, an enormous racing wall of metal. The small enclave we were hiding in bounced and rattled as if it would shiver to pieces around us.

Then the train powered by. The pitch of the noise shifted. The light began to fade. The roar got softer and softer.

Gone. Quiet. We could hear the clicks of the tracks again and the distant rumble of other trains, further away.

I looked around at the little hole we were in.

'What's this?'

'For workmen,' Mike said. 'So they don't get run over in the tunnels.'

'Nice,' I said. 'How'd you know it was here?'

'I didn't.'

He moved out. Bowing my head beneath the alcove's lintel, I came after him, back into the tunnel.

Out of breath and shaken, we walked along now toward the tunnel's end. I have to admit, I kept looking back over my shoulder, afraid I'd see another train coming down on us. But, no.

Up ahead, beyond the tunnel, there were other trains going by. A glow would grow bright, pass over the tunnel walls and then fade away, then another glow would rise and fade, and another, as the trains moved in the distance. But there were no more trains in our tunnel. We made it to the end and stepped out into another open underground arcade.

This one was even bigger than the last – a vast space of criss-crossing tracks with small lights in the walls and large columns rising to towering heights above. It looked like part of a buried city, a mall maybe or some other place where people had once come to meet and talk and shop before it was sealed up underground. Now, there were only the deep shadows over everything – shadows suddenly split by a train passing out of one tunnel, through the arcade, and disappearing into another. Then the shadows sank down again and the tunnel became dark and quiet, with only the distant rattle of trains and the clicks of the switches, and the red lights turning green then red again.

'Which way now?' I said.

Mike pointed across the arcade toward yet another tunnel. 'That way. That'll take us to the intersection I'm looking for.'

We took a single step – and then there was a high-pitched shriek – a shrieking whistle as a train shot out of a tunnel in front of us. Its headlight shot through the shadowy cavern, rolling off one column, illuminating the filthy tiles of the wall. I saw the scrambling rats. I felt the stirring air.

And I saw something else, too.

Just for a moment, as the headlight went past me – in the single instant before the train cut off my view – I caught a glimpse of a face – a human face – moving in the darkness on the far side of the arcade. An oval of white. Two eyes gleaming with reflected light.

'Mike!' I said. 'There's someone there.'

But the rumble of the train drowned out my voice. He couldn't hear me.

Then the train torpedoed past, through the arcade. For a second, I was blinded by the shift from light to darkness.

I stared at the spot where I'd seen that face. I couldn't see anything there now.

'Mike,' I said again, my voice softer.

But, before I could say another word, there was a crack echoing off the walls of the arcade. There was a gout of flame on the far side of the criss-crossing tracks. I felt a breath on my cheek. I felt a sting as I was hit by a fragment of tile flying off the wall behind me.

'Get down!' Mike shouted, diving for the darkness.

We were under fire.

Chapter Thirty-three

Gunfight

I hurled myself to the earth as another shot echoed through the great underground hall. The dirt and gravel in front of me exploded as the bullet hit. I was so frantic to roll out of the way, I didn't watch where I was going. When I stopped rolling, my nose was inches from the side of the third rail. Another turn and a blast of current would've snuffed me out.

I took a breath to steady myself, edged away from the rail and reached into my shoulder holster.

I drew out the 9mm and pointed it into the dark.

A glow was growing through the arcade. A train was coming out of one of the tunnels. In the light from the headlight, I could make out four figures moving on the far side of the arcade. I turned my gun in their direction.

There was an explosion and a blast of flame beside me. Mike. Lying on the track, he'd spotted the four figures too and opened fire. I heard a scream from across the expanse. The light in the arcade grew brighter as the train neared. I could see there were only three figures now. They all opened fire at once, the rapid explosions of their guns visible through the shifting shadows thrown by the nearing headlight.

'Move it, Charlie!' Mike shouted.

He was on his feet, dodging over the tracks with his body bent low. I did what he did, hopping over the third rail, moving quickly toward the cover of one of the columns.

I got behind the column just as another round of shots went off on the far side of the arcade. Tiles and stone flew off the column in a white blast as I ducked behind it. Then I peeked out again and fired into the dark. To be honest, I was too pumped full of adrenalin and fear to take careful aim. I just sort of fired blindly. I knew I hadn't hit anyone.

Mike fired, ducking from one column to another. The three gunmen fired back.

Then the train shot out of the tunnel to my left – and it was heading right for me.

I had only a second before it ran me down. I rushed to get out of the way – and, as I did, I came out from behind the column, exposing myself to gunfire. Sure enough, the three gunmen spotted me and their guns cracked through the arcade. I thought I felt something whistle by my arm. Then the train went roaring by, towering over me, its windows flashing bright above me as they went past. The huge machine cut me off from the gunmen. I took advantage of that, running along beside it, changing location while I couldn't be seen.

Then the train raced out of the arcade and disappeared into another tunnel. I crouched and leveled my gun at the place where the gunmen had been. I hesitated. In the sudden dark, I couldn't see much of anything. I expected them to start shooting again any second. But they didn't.

Then Mike was right beside me. 'They're on the move,' he said, breathless. 'This way.'

He raced off across the arcade. I raced after him, leaping the tracks. We reached the far side and there was the gunman Mike had shot. He lay on his side in a pool of blood, dead, his eyes open and staring into the underground darkness.

I hesitated a second, staring at the fallen man's face. I recognized him – remembered him from my days of training in the forest compound. He was one of the Homelanders, for sure.

I stepped over the body and moved after Mike. I caught up with him in a long corridor, a broader tunnel this time in which four tracks ran side by side with columns between them. I peered ahead through the darkness, trying to make out the remaining Homelanders. I didn't see them.

But they were there all right. As we moved further into the tunnel, there was another round of gunshots. There was a whine and spattering cracks as bullets smacked into the tunnel wall. The guns were off to our left now, on another set of tracks. Mike and I stayed low, moving toward the columns. I positioned myself behind one. He got behind another.

I leaned there, my heart beating hard. The situation felt surreal, like a nightmare. Above us in the city, millions of revelers were laughing through the chilly night, celebrating the new year. Here, right below them, we were trading bullets with a bunch of terrorists moving toward their target over the train tracks. Some part of me thought I would soon wake up, find myself back in my cell in Abingdon, or better yet find myself at home, the entire experience of the Homelanders a dream.

Another shot blew that idea away in a big hurry. The bullet smacked into the side of the column I was hiding behind and threw up another blast of chips and dust.

I felt a wind wash over me again – heard a rumble. I looked to my left and saw a train heading into our tunnel. It was traveling on one of the tracks between me and the Homelanders. I glanced at Mike, hiding behind the column next to me. His eyes were bright with the reflected headlight. He saw the train coming, too, about to cut us off from the gunmen on the other side of the tunnel.

He rolled out from behind the column and fired in the direction of the Homelanders. Three gouts of flame answered back and the bullets zinged past us. Mike ducked back behind the column again and nodded at me, his face growing brighter as the headlight came near.

'These guys were stationed to pin us down,' he called to me over the noise of the train. 'Prince and the poison are moving to their target while we shoot it out. We gotta end this, Charlie. Now.'

Just then, the train fired into the tunnel, cutting us off from the Homelanders – and on the instant, without another word, Mike moved. He curled out from behind the column and started running across the tracks, heading straight for the train as it barreled past.

I went after him. The earth shook under my feet as the huge beast of a machine stampeded through the tunnel, its lighted windows right above me, its flashing sides inches from me. Mike knelt down, his gun leveled. I knelt down, too. I leveled my gun, too. I didn't know the plan but I figured if I followed Mike I couldn't go far wrong.

Then the train flashed past and the Homelander gunmen were right across the tracks from us. Mike and I started firing at the same moment. A man screamed. An answering gun went off. I saw the flame pointed toward the ceiling. I saw the man's silhouette as he reeled backwards, hit.

Then, to my absolute shock, Mike leapt forward, firing as he moved. He pumped bullets from his gun rapid-fire and the gunmen fired back. Then I heard the trigger click and I knew Mike's 9mm was empty.

But by then, Mike was right on top of the two remaining gunmen. One lowered a gun at him and Mike kicked it from his hand. The other shot at him – so close I didn't see how he could miss. But Mike seemed unhurt. He grabbed the guy's wrist and twisted it. I heard the bone snap where I was, heard the man let out a shriek of agony before his body crumpled to the tracks.

I ran toward Mike. But, before I was anywhere near, the first man – the last Homelander gunman in the tunnel – leapt on Mike and the two struggled together.

It was a quick fight. I saw their shadows intermingle as the Homelander moved in for the kill. Then I saw their shadows fly apart as Mike knocked him back.

Then Mike went at him in a flurry of sweeping strikes, his feet shooting out in a series of kicks so quick I could barely see them, his hands sweeping around to chop at the attacker even as the attacker was reeling back. Then Mike let out a loud 'Kee-yai!' and his fist smashed into the gun-man's chin so hard, the guy actually flew up into the air like something in a movie, leaving his feet and landing on his backside before tipping over sideways on to the track, where he lay still.

It was over so quickly that I was just reaching Mike as the last man fell.

Then I was beside my old sensei in the tunnel. He stood there, breathing hard, looking around.

He lifted his chin, pointing along the tracks.

'That way,' he said. 'I don't think there'll be many of them left. You'll be all right.'

I gave a breathless laugh. 'Yeah, well, seeing as you just took out two guys with guns, I'd say we have them out-numbered.'

There was a little quirk in Mike's moustache: a barely visible smile. 'Good thing I taught you so well, I guess.'

'What do you mean?'

'Looks like you're gonna be on your own from here.'

I started to smile. I figured it was some kind of joke. Then I caught the look in Mike's eyes and I realized he wasn't joking at all. I stood there staring stupidly. Finally, I got it. My eyes went down to where Mike's hand pressed against his side. His fingers were already dark. With grime, I thought, and then I realized – no. There was blood pumping out of his side, pouring over his hand.

'Mike – Mike, you're hit,' I said.

'No kidding. Pretty sharp observation for a chucklehead, chucklehead.' He gave a grunt of pain and staggered where he stood. He reached out and took hold of my shoulder. I grabbed on to his arm, trying to hold him up. But before I could get a good grip, he sank down to his knees, too heavy for me to hold.

I went down on my knees beside him. 'It's all right, Mike. I got you. I'll bring you topside, we'll find an ambulance.'

He shook his head. 'No way. No time. Gotta keep going. Gotta stop Prince.'

'That's crazy, Mike.' I took hold of him under the arm. I tried to lift him to his feet. He wouldn't let me. 'Mike, you're hurt,' I said. 'You need help. You're hurt bad.'

He grabbed the front of my jacket, yanked my face so close to his I could feel his breath on me. 'You think I don't know how bad I'm hurt?'

'Let me go. I'll get help.'

'No, you won't. You'll go after Prince. You'll stop him before he sets off that gas, before he kills a million people.'

'I'm not gonna just leave you down here.'

'Wrong again, pal. Yes, you are.'

'Mike . . .'

He shook me – weakly, though – I could feel the strength going out of him. 'Listen to me. You said . . . You told me . . . You said you would do what you had to do.'

'That's not what I meant . . .'

'What did you mean? You meant you'd do what you had to do if it was fun, if it was nice, if you approved?'

'No, I—'

'If it meant killing a bad guy or winning a fight?'

'I just meant—'

'*This* is what you have to do, Charlie. You have to leave me here. You have to let me try to save myself while you go after them and try to save everybody else. This is what you have to do.'

I opened my mouth. I tried to talk but I felt like there was a sneaker stuck in my throat. I swallowed it down. 'I can't, Mike,' I managed to say finally. 'I can't just leave you.'

'Don't you tell me that.' Mike's hand sank down. He slumped weakly where he sat. I looked down at his side. The blood was still burbling out of the bullet wound there. 'Don't tell me you can't,' he murmured. 'I taught you. I trained you, Charlie. If you can't do what you have to do, I'm a failure. I'm dying for nothing here.'

'What do you mean, "dying"? You can't die.'

He tried to laugh but he didn't have the strength. 'Everybody dies, chucklehead. It's the first rule of the game. Now listen to me: I'm gonna be all right.'

'Mike . . .'

'I mean it. You and me, chucklehead, we never talk about the faith stuff much. The way I see it, there's not much to say. But you know where I stand. I did my best to live true, and whatever happens next, I'm gonna be fine. All right? So what

I need, the thing I really need, is for you to go hunt those terrorists down and stop them from killing a lot of innocent—' He didn't finish the sentence. The pain hit him and he cried out. I felt my whole body go rigid as if the pain were my pain instead of his.

When he could talk again, Mike said weakly, 'There's no more time to talk about this. You told me you'd do what you had to do, Charlie. Now do it.'

I had to bite my lip to keep from crying. I wanted to answer him, to protest, to say something, but there was nothing for me to say. I knew he was right. I knew there was no time to do both: help Mike and stop Prince from doing what he was going to do. We were down below the city and no one knew we were here. If this job was going to get finished, I was the one who was going to have to finish it – alone.

I stood up. I looked down at where Mike sat on the ground, resting on one hand. He was between two tracks so at least the trains couldn't get him. The three gunmen he'd taken out lay splayed all around him. Two lay very still. One, unconscious, groaned a little and stirred. But his arm was twisted in a weird position, and I knew he wasn't going to come around any time soon.

'Don't worry,' said Mike. 'I still have my weapon.' He tried to lift the gun to show me, but his hand sank back down to the ground. 'I got a spare mag, too. I can take care of myself.'

'Right,' I managed to answer back, pretending I believed it.

A train rumbled towards us out of the distance one track

over. Rats scrambled past us. One of them crawled right over Mike's extended leg. He didn't even have the strength to kick it off. Instead, he busied himself with one of the bodies of the Homelanders. He stripped off the guy's windbreaker. He bunched it up and pressed it to his side, trying to staunch the flow of blood.

'What are you waiting for?' he said to me. He had to raise his voice to be heard over the growing rumble of the approaching train.

'I don't . . .' I started to say. But the train was too loud now. I knew he wouldn't hear me. I wanted to tell him, *I don't know what to do.*

The train roared by, the light from its windows flashing over us. It gave me a good look at Mike's pain-wracked face. Then it was gone, the rattle of it fading.

'You'll figure it out,' Mike said, as if he had read my mind. 'You're not alone, Charlie. You're never alone.'

I nodded. 'I'll be back,' I said. 'I'll be back for you. I swear it.'

Mike smiled, a real smile so I could see his teeth beneath his 'tache. 'I'll be here, chucklehead. You can count on it. Now, go.'

I wanted to say something else, anything else, anything to hold off the moment when I had to leave him. But how could I ever say what had to be said? How could I thank him – for teaching me, for believing in me for leading me? Even for this – maybe especially for this. How could I ever thank him for forcing me to go on alone?

'I'll see you, Mike,' I said finally.

'Yes you will. Godspeed, chucklehead.'

I nodded.

Then I left him there.

Chapter Thirty-four

Alone

I had never felt so hopeless, so afraid. I'd been tortured, shot at, beaten, locked up. I'd been running for my life so long I'd almost forgotten what it was like to live without being hunted. But all that time, there'd been something in me, something that lifted me over fear, that never let me sink to the final level of despair. The bad guys were after me, OK, but at least I knew where I was going. I just had to get away, stay alive, prove my innocence, take the next step and the next until I found my way home.

But this wasn't like that. It wasn't about me. It wasn't even about Mike, though I could barely stand to think of him alone and bleeding back there in the dark behind me.

This was about all those people up above me, up there in the city, thousands and thousands and thousands of ordinary people, coming together to celebrate the new year – and all of them in danger, their lives under threat. All their lives depended on me – me alone – and what I did next.

See, all this while, all night long, I'd just been following

Mike. Well, sure I was – Mike was my teacher, my sensei. He always knew what to do, where to go. He could handle anything. I was glad to follow him. I'd been his student since I was a little kid.

But now . . . now he was gone. Now it was just me down here – just me standing between a million people and total, absolute catastrophe. What if I couldn't stop it? You know? What if I couldn't even find Prince? I mean, I hadn't studied the maps like Mike had. What if I took a wrong turn and just got myself lost in the tunnels and wandered around like an idiot while Prince let his poisoned gas loose into the city? I could already see the headlines in my mind:

Guy Acts Stupid While Millions Die.

The rest of my life, that would be all I would think about. How I couldn't make it without Mike to lead me. How I failed everyone at the most evil hour of the most desperate day.

I hurried through the tunnel, through the shadows, the fear of failure like a sickness in me, making my breath short, my stomach weak. I could feel the sweat pouring off me. I could feel the dampness of my hand against the handle of the gun. It wasn't just the running and fighting that made me sweat. This was a cold sweat, an anxiety sweat. It was the sweat of fear.

I came out of the tunnel into another great arcade, a vast expanse of emptiness and columns and shadows. There were tunnels all around me, tracks disappearing into deeper darkness.

I stopped at the edge of the place. I looked from one exit to another. I felt the hopelessness like a bottomless pit inside me, the fear like a hand tightening on my throat.

Where was I supposed to go now? Which tunnel? Which way?

'You're not alone, Charlie,' I whispered to myself – as if I were Mike, as if I were Mike talking to me. 'You're never alone.'

I felt my heart reach out desperately into the darkness.

Help me, I thought.

Almost as if it were an answer to my prayer, a train shot out of one of the tunnels, the light glaring in my eyes as it headed my way. I quickly moved to the right, off the tracks and edged away further into the arcade. The train barreled by to my left and then disappeared into the tunnel behind me.

It vanished into darkness. And it turned out my prayer had not been answered at all. There I was, just as before, and I had no more clue which way to go now than I had when the train appeared. My lips were still dry with fear. My stomach was still empty with hopelessness.

Then I saw the way.

It was because I'd moved. I'd shifted position to get out of the path of the train. Now I was looking directly down one of the tunnels that exited the arcade. As I stood trying to figure out my next move, something blinked down there: a light – more than one light – several lights with different colors, blinking and shifting in the shadows again and again.

Instinctively, I started moving toward that light. After only a few steps, I understood what it was.

It was light coming into the tunnels from the outside – electric light of some kind, maybe neon lights – something that was blinking and shifting up there.

Times Square! I thought.

Of course. Times Square, where the New Year's ball came down, where the greatest concentration of people would be. If Prince was going to release gas into Times Square, he'd have to go somewhere with an opening on to the street.

I started to run. I crossed the arcade and headed for the tunnel.

It was a narrow passage with only one track running through it. The minute I stepped into it, I saw what I was looking for.

Up ahead, there was a narrow platform and tiled walls, illuminated by dim lights. It looked as if they had begun to build a station here but never finished it.

The colored lights blinked and shifted on the walls and I lifted my eyes. There, above the platform, there were two grates in the high ceiling. Through the grates, I could see the city. A solid mass of people was passing overhead. I could hear noisemakers and shouts and an enormous whisper of human motion. I could hear music in the distance, as if a live performance were in progress. And I caught glimpses of lights: big lighted signs, jumbo TV screens, massive shifting images that sent their moving, blinking glow down here into this dark, underground world.

And, finally, I saw Prince.

He was dressed all in black so that he blended with the shadows of the station. But a track switch clicked somewhere and a red signal light in the tunnel turned green and the green light picked his moving silhouette out of the surrounding darkness.

Prince was at the far end of the station platform. He was at a ladder embedded in the wall there: a long, long workman's ladder leading up to the high ceiling and the grates maybe ten stories above. He was just about to begin the climb. As he took hold of the ladder, I saw he had a knapsack on his back. I knew he must have the Cylon Orange device in there.

A breath of foul wind blew over me. A rumble sounded in the near distance. A train was coming, headed for the tunnel.

'Prince!' I shouted.

He glanced over and saw me. His eyes flashed as they caught the light from the oncoming train. He didn't hesitate. He started his climb.

I ran over to the platform, grabbed hold of the edge and hauled myself up. I leveled my gun at Prince.

'Prince!' I shouted again. 'Stop, or I'll shoot!'

He didn't stop, not even for a second. He kept climbing.

The rumble of the train grew louder. The glow of its headlight started to spread over the tracks below me.

I took aim.

Then a man stepped out of the shadows and pressed a gun to my head.

I spun even before the barrel touched me, sweeping my

gun hand around to knock his gun away. Good thing I was fast: he was already pulling the trigger. The gun went off with a deafening blast but the bullet went wild as his gun went flying. I lowered the barrel of my gun to his face, ready to shoot, ready to kill him then and there so I could stop Prince.

But he was fast, too. He spun away and back-kicked me in the gut. I staggered and he kicked again – a high kick at my wrist this time – knocking the gun out of my hand.

He was a big man, blocky, blond and stupid-looking, but he moved like a bolt of lightning. He jabbed his stiffened fingers at my throat. I dodged to the side and grabbed his arm. I elbowed him in the face, crushing his nose in a blast of blood, but it barely slowed him. He wrapped his arms around me and charged to the edge of the platform, carrying me with him.

We both went over the side together, falling down to the tracks into the path of the oncoming train.

The impact of the ground broke the big man's hold on me. I jumped to my feet – and saw the headlight bearing down on me, seconds away. The Homelander was up just as quick, his shadow blocking the light. The rumble of the train filled the tunnel. A warning whistle screamed, deafening.

Desperation filled me. All I could think was, *If I die here, a big chunk of the city dies with me.*

I leapt for the platform. It was a bad move. The Homelander threw himself at me – grabbed me. I elbowed him again. He wouldn't let go. The train bore down on both of us as we struggled.

I twisted around and hit the big man with the web of my hand, right under the chin. He gagged. His arms lost their strength. With the power of terror, I hurled him away from me. He staggered backwards a few steps – and suddenly stood bolt upright. Caught in the glare from the onrushing train, he froze in position, trembling as if in fear.

But it wasn't fear. He had backed into the third rail. It was the voltage that had frozen him there. He was staring at me, trembling. But in fact, he was already dead.

The train punched into the station, heading straight at me. I turned and threw myself at the platform again, hauling myself up.

I felt the whisper of death on my sleeve as the train rushed by me. But I was already rolling across the platform, safe. The next second, the train was gone.

The Homelander was gone, too. Not a sign of him. I guess the train hit him and carried him off – but I didn't have time to figure it out now.

I looked across the platform and saw Prince. He was almost halfway up the ladder, moving quickly, steadily toward the grate that opened up into Times Square, pausing only a moment to reach behind him and shift the pack he had strapped to his back.

I climbed to my feet and raced after him.

Chapter Thirty-five

On the Ladder

There was no time to recover my gun. Once Prince reached the top of the ladder, once he reached the grate, there was nothing to stop him from starting his device, charging those canisters and releasing the gas. I ran as I'd never run before, straining every muscle with an effort that sent me tearing across the platform at top speed.

I leapt for the ladder and started hauling myself up. If I was exhausted, if I was weak, if I was battered, I no longer felt it, any of it. I just felt the need to move, to climb, to go, to reach him, to stop him.

As fast as Prince climbed, I climbed faster. I closed the distance quickly. I saw his figure getting larger up above, framed against the shifting light of the signs and TV screens blinking down over us. The music played louder as I got closer to the surface, a happy rock tune making a bizarre, jaunty counterpoint to our desperate chase.

Prince scrambled toward the lights and music and I scrambled after him.

At first, I don't think he even knew I was there. I think he must've assumed the big thug below had taken care of me. Maybe he saw us go on to the tracks together and figured I was done for. I don't know. But for the longest time, he didn't even look down. He didn't see me coming.

I kept scrambling up the ladder, my teeth gritted and bared. Higher and higher until the floor was practically invisible beneath me, a blur of shadows, ten stories down.

Prince climbed and I climbed faster. I got closer and closer to him. Prince was now about five rungs from the top, moments from reaching the grate. Below, I had come within two rungs of him.

I guess, at that point, he sensed my presence because, finally, he looked down and saw me.

I was close enough to see his reaction, even in the dim light. His normally cool, sophisticated expression changed completely as surprise made his eyes go wide. My guess must've been right: he must've thought I was dead. The sight of me there, right beneath him, clearly caught him totally off guard.

He let go of the ladder with one hand. The hand went to his belt – a gun. If he had time to pull it, I'd be dead, an easy target. There was nowhere to duck or dodge on the ladder and, if I let go now, it was a long way down. It'd be a miracle to survive slamming into the platform from ten stories up.

Fear gave me the extra burst I needed to close the final gap between us. I came up under Prince's feet. His body blocked the rungs above me. I grabbed the side of the ladder with one hand and grabbed his leg with the other. I pulled myself up another rung and another.

Prince cursed and tried to kick me off him. I lost my hold on his leg. I swung out over the abyss, still holding the ladder with one hand.

Prince drew his gun and pointed it down at me. I hauled myself upward and reached for him, wrapping my fingers around his wrist, twisting it. He tried to yank away, but I pulled myself up further and got some leverage on him, pinning him against the ladder. I smacked his gun hand against the wall – once, twice, three times. Finally, he dropped the weapon. It went spinning down and down into the shadows.

Above me now, I could hear the voices of the New Year's revelers. I could hear horns and noisemakers and people shouting, singing and laughing. I could hear the live band as if it were right down the street. The glare of the jumbo TV and the blinking neon shone in my eyes. I caught a glimpse of a gigantic smiling face – some movie star on a billboard or something – grinning down at me through the grate.

Then Prince tore his arm free of my grasp and hammered blindly at my face with his fist. The blow struck me high on the head – it dazed me – but I wouldn't let go; I wouldn't back off. I grabbed his backpack and pulled myself up behind him. My feet lost their purchase on the ladder and dangled free. I clung to Prince's pack with one hand, and to the outside of the ladder with the other. Prince tried to throw me off, twisting, hitting out with one hand.

Turning, he saw my hand on the ladder. He grabbed at it,

starting to pry my fingers loose. I could feel myself losing my grip. So I let go of the ladder and grabbed him. Now I was holding on to Prince's backpack with both hands, my feet dangling in the air. If I let go, if I lost my hold, I'd drop like a stone and he'd be free to release his poison into the city above me.

Using all that was left of my strength, I pulled myself up, climbing over him. I released his pack with one hand, and grabbed him by the collar. I struggled to get a foothold on the ladder but couldn't find a place, couldn't get around his body. Prince, meanwhile, fought ferociously, trying to pry me off him with one hand, while clinging to the ladder with the other.

I continued to climb up Prince's body until I could wrap my arm around his throat. I pulled the arm tight, choking him as he tried to pull away, thrashing his free hand around at me, trying to gouge my eyes.

An idea came to me now – so clear in the midst of that frantic fight, it was almost like a voice speaking quietly into my mind. Prince had one hand on the ladder as he tried to knock me off with the other. There's a nerve in the back of the hand – I learned this in karate – Mike taught it to me. If you drill that nerve with a knuckle, just right, it causes a lot of pain, enough pain to break any hold. If I drilled the back of Prince's hand with my knuckle, he would let go of the ladder and with my arm around his throat, I could pull him off. We would both go down, both fall to the platform below. We would both almost surely be killed, but the threat would be over, the city would be safe.

Here's a funny thing: you'd think I'd be afraid. Of falling, I mean. Of dying, most likely, down there in that abandoned station. But the reverse was true, weirdly enough. I'd been afraid all this time up till now, but now I wasn't. Until this moment – until the moment I realized that I could end this – I'd been really terrified that I might fail, that I might do the wrong thing and get lost or killed or something and let Prince succeed with his plan and let Mike down. But now – now that fear was gone. I had him. I knew I had him. I knew it was over. There was nothing left but to deliver this final strike the way Mike taught me and bring Prince down with me to the ground.

Everybody dies, chucklehead. It's the first rule of the game.

I wasn't afraid.

One arm around Prince's throat, I lifted my free hand, setting the knuckle for a piercing blow.

I did my best to live true and, whatever happens next, I'm gonna be fine.

I hesitate only half a second. The questions flashed through my mind: What about me? Had I done my best? Had I tried to live true? The questions came and images came – images of the people I knew: my parents, my friends, Beth – Beth, most of all. Would they be angry at me for leaving them? Would they understand? Would they know why I had done what I'd done?

All that in half a second. Then I drove the strike into the back of Prince's hand.

He cried out and lost his hold on the ladder. I dragged him backward and we fell.

Prince let out a shriek. We tumbled over once in the shadowy air. I saw the lights of Times Square through the grate above me, falling away. I heard the music of the world fading.

I was so committed to the fall, so ready to do what I had to do, that I almost didn't think to snatch at the ladder as it went past.

But then I did. I reached out wildly. My fingers touched metal and I grabbed hold. I had a rung of the ladder. I dropped and held there, and the jolt nearly pulled my arm out of its socket. I lost my hold on Prince but he clutched at my sleeve and caught it. I grabbed his wrist. The two of us dangled there, far above the platform, me holding on to a ladder rung, Prince holding on to me. I tried to get my feet back on the ladder but Prince's weight was pulling me straight down, pulling my fingers off the rung so that I could not move.

I looked down at him, straining to keep my grip on the ladder, straining to keep my grip on him. He looked up at me, his eyes desperate, pleading.

'Drop the pack!' I shouted down at him.

He shouted a curse back at me, his eyes hot with rage and hatred.

His weight kept pulling me, pulling me. My fingers kept slipping off the ladder rung, little by little.

'Drop it, Prince, and I'll try to pull you up!'

His answer was the same.

I was losing my grip. I couldn't hold on to him any longer. I shook my head at him.

'No!' Prince shouted – a cry of pure terror.

But another second and I would fall. I let go of him – yanked my arm away. I grabbed hold of the ladder with both hands and clung on.

I saw Prince fall, turning in air. He had time to scream out once more – then his body hit the platform far below.

It made an awful sound.

Chapter Thirty-six

The End

I climbed down the ladder as quickly as I could. I went to Prince and stood over him. He was still alive, but his body was twisted in a strange position and I knew he would not last long. He lay completely still, staring up at me. Only his lips were moving. He was trying to speak. I knelt down next to him. Put my ear close to his lips and listened.

'We will . . . destroy you . . .' he whispered.

Startled, I turned to look in his eyes. They still burned hot with rage and hatred. If he could've moved, I think he would've spent his last breath trying to strangle me.

It was a terrible way to die, I thought, feeling like that, being like that. That much anger: it must be like having acid in your heart. God, save me from it, I thought. God save me from ever hating anything or anyone that much.

I put my hand on Prince's shoulder. To be honest, I almost felt sorry for the guy. I did feel sorry for him. Only God knew what had made his life what it was, what had filled him with that kind of passion for destruction. Only God knew and only

God could judge. I had stopped him from killing the people above me. That was the job that had fallen to me; not to hate him, just to stop him. The job was done now. It was enough.

He died a few seconds later. I watched him go. I heard his last breath rattle in his throat. I watched the life leave his eyes. Anyone who's ever seen that happen will tell you, you can almost see the soul depart. It made me wonder, *Did the world look different to him now that he was gone? Was the hatred gone too?* I bet if we could see the world from the perspective of the dead, it would look a whole lot different. I bet no one would ever hurt anyone then.

I knelt there and worked the backpack off Prince's corpse. I opened the flap and looked inside. I could see the solid black object in there, the thing they called the device, I guess. I closed the pack, and looped its strap over my shoulders.

I had to go. I had to get back to Mike. If he was still alive – and he had to be still alive, he had to be – I would get him help, get him to a hospital, if I had to carry him the whole way.

Toting Prince's backpack, I lowered myself off the platform, down to the train tracks. I began jogging back the way I came, back toward Mike. I knew I had to hurry, but I was so exhausted, I stumbled every other step. My mouth was hanging open. My vision was blurred.

I stepped out of the tunnel into the arcade and a light shone in my eyes. A train, I thought. Heading for me.

But it wasn't a train. Because then another light shone at me out of the darkness and another.

What now? I thought wearily. If there were any Homelanders left, I was finished. I couldn't fight anymore.

A voice shouted at me, 'Drop the pack, West! Put it down and put your hands up!'

I stopped and stood there, confused, squinting into the glare of the bobbing lights coming toward me.

'Who's there?' I said – I barely had the strength to speak. 'Who are you?'

'Police,' said one voice.

'FBI,' said another.

'Put the pack down, West!' yet another voice called. 'Put your hands up!'

Blinking with exhaustion, I slipped the pack off my shoulder and dropped it on to the tracks. I lifted my hands in the air so they could see them. I stood there, swaying unsteadily on my feet.

A moment later, seven men came out of the darkness, all of them carrying flashlights, all of them carrying guns. Four of the men were in uniform – New York Police Department – NYPD. Three other guys were in suits and ties. One of the NYPD patrolmen came forward, took my raised hands and brought them around behind my back. I felt the cold metal of the handcuffs as they snapped around my wrists.

'Mike,' I said. 'My friend – Mike. He was shot. He's hurt.'

One of the plain-clothes guys, a tall, broad-shouldered,

balding man, nodded at me. 'Yeah, we found him. Looks like he took a few people with him.'

'He's dead?'

'Not yet, he's not. He was breathing when we got to him, anyway. He's being carried out to an EMS unit.'

'Alive,' I murmured dully. The word was like a small flame of hope flaring inside me.

The balding man nodded. 'So far, yeah. He's still alive.'

Another of the plain-clothes men, a small, narrow, red-haired guy, said, 'Here it is.' He was kneeling on the tracks, looking in the backpack. 'Looks like what they said. We better get the bomb squad down here.'

Then, 'We got a dead one!' someone shouted from behind me in the tunnel.

'That's Prince,' I told the balding guy. 'He was one of the Homelanders. He was trying—'

'We know who he was. We know what he was trying to do,' Balding Guy said. He stepped forward to where I stood with my hands cuffed behind me. He put his hand on my shoulder. 'Your friend, Rose, told us.'

Dazed, I could only look at him. Then I said, 'You mean, you believe him? You finally believe him?'

Balding Guy gave a hollow laugh. 'I guess we do now, don't we?'

For a second, I couldn't take this in. I couldn't comprehend what it meant. Then I did. It meant that it was over. Finally over. People knew the truth now. They understood what had happened, what I'd done, why I'd done it. I wasn't alone anymore.

My vision blurred as my eyes filled with tears. *Not alone. Never alone.*

The plain-clothes man with the red hair glanced at the balding plain-clothes man.

'Looks like this kid just saved the entire city of New York,' Red Hair said.

Balding Guy smiled wryly and nodded. Lifting his chin to the patrolman beside me, he said, 'Take those cuffs off him, will you?'

I felt my hands come free as the cuffs were removed. I rubbed my wrists to take the tingling out of them.

My voice was unsteady. 'Does this mean . . . ?' I swallowed hard. 'Does this mean I won't have to go back to prison?'

Balding Guy let out another thick laugh. He glanced at Red Hair. Red Hair shook his head, smiling.

'I don't write the laws, kid,' Balding Guy said. 'And I can't make any promises. But, as far as I'm concerned, you deserve a medal and a parade.' He slapped me on the shoulder again. 'Happy New Year,' he said.

Epilogue

I was lying in my bed with the covers pulled up around my chin. The mattress was soft and I was warm and comfortable. It was just about time for breakfast. I could smell the eggs cooking in the kitchen below. Any minute now, I knew my mom was going to call me from the bottom of the stairs. I would get dressed and go down and find my father and my sister waiting for me at the table. Then, after we ate, it would be time to head off to school. My friends would be waiting for me. And Beth . . .

'West.'

I sat up straight, coming out of my dream. Confused, I looked around me. I was sitting in a plastic chair, one of a row of plastic chairs bolted to the wall of a tiled hallway. A nurse walked by me – then another, this one pushing an old man in a wheelchair.

My back ached; I shifted. I looked at myself. I was wearing a fresh track suit. I had a bandage on my arm. I could feel another bandage wrapped around my ribs. I lifted my hand and touched yet another bandage, this one on my forehead.

I remembered: I was in the hall of a hospital in Manhattan. It was New Year's Day – no, the day after New Year's: January 2nd. I'd been in the hospital for two days now. I'd been bandaged and examined by doctors and nurses. I'd been questioned and interrogated by agents and police. I'd been sleeping – in beds, in chairs – anywhere I could find. And I'd been dreaming – the same old dream – about my life, my old life, back home, back in Spring Hill. I was only slowly beginning to accept the fact that, no matter what happened next, that old life was over. It was gone for good.

'West?'

Still dazed with sleep and exhaustion, I lifted my eyes to the voice that had awakened me: Rose. He was standing over me, next to my chair. He was leaning on a crutch. His left leg was in a cast. There was a bandage high on his balding head.

'Rose . . .'

'You all right? You fell asleep again.'

It was all coming back to me. The prison break. The flight to New York. Patel. The plane crash. The chase through the subway and . . .

'Mike,' I said. I stood up, trying to shake my head clear. 'How's Mike?' He had been in surgery all yesterday. It had been bad – tough. His heart had stopped once on the operating table. But there was life in him still – a lot of life. He'd fought his way back.

Without a word, Rose tilted his head, beckoning me to follow him. He hobbled away from me, down the tiled hall. There were policemen, I saw, stationed along the wall. A lot of them, it seemed like. Every few doors, another patrolman, standing guard. They had been here since I arrived. They'd been watching me every second. I hadn't been allowed to leave the place. I hadn't even been allowed to call home. I was still a convicted killer, after all. And, even if Rose could clear that up, I was still a fugitive. Were they going to take me back to Abingdon Prison eventually? I didn't know. I didn't have any idea what was going to happen next.

But right now, I couldn't think about that. I wouldn't think about it. I had to think about Mike, about whether Mike was going to live or die.

Now, as I followed Rose, I didn't say anything. I didn't ask any questions. I was afraid to hear the answers, to be honest. For all I knew, Mike had already passed away while I slept. A sense of dread gnawed at my stomach. I heard Mike's voice in my mind.

I did my best to live true and, whatever happens next, I'm gonna be fine.

I believed that. Yes, I did. But I wasn't ready for him to go.

Rose hobbled his way to a door. Another patrolman stood outside it. He held the door open for us.

I followed Rose into a small room with a single bed by the window. Winter daylight streamed in through the glass and steel towers across the way. The light fell on Mike. He lay on the bed. There were a lot of wires and tubes and stuff around him: a tube ran into his arm; a wire was attached to his chest; an oxygen mask over his face. It was kind of scary to see such a big tough guy looking so weak and helpless there.

But alive. At least Mike was still alive. He was breathing steadily and the heart-rate gizmo by his bed showed all his vital signs strong and steady.

I glanced at Rose. He lifted his chin, telling me to go closer to the bed. I stepped up close and looked down into Mike's face. His eyes were closed but his expression was peaceful.

As I looked down at him, Mike's eyes came open suddenly. They shifted and he saw me. He smiled behind his oxygen mask. His hand lifted weakly to his face and pulled the mask down from his mouth.

'Chucklehead,' he whispered.

My legs went unsteady. There was a chair nearby. I pulled it to me and sat down. I reached out and took Mike's hand, careful not to disturb the pulse monitor on his fingertip.

'Hey, Mike,' I managed to say. 'Long time no see.'

His eyes fluttered closed and opened again. 'That's twice those Isalmist guys have shot me,' he murmured slowly. 'Next time, I might get seriously annoyed.'

I started to laugh, then I had to cover my eyes with my hand. Mike pushed the oxygen mask up over his mouth again and closed his eyes and rested.

I sat there with him a long time. After a while, I guess I must've slept again. It seemed like, the next thing I knew, Rose was waking me up, his hand on my shoulder.

'You got a phone call, West,' he said.

I followed him again down the hospital hallways, past the watchful patrolmen to an office in a quiet corner.

It was a small office with just a small window looking out on an airshaft and a dirty brick wall. There was a desk in there with a phone on it. There wasn't much else.

'Just pick it up and press line one,' said Rose.

He walked out and left me alone.

I went to the desk. I picked up the phone. There was a button on it with a light blinking. I pressed the button.

'Hello?' I said. 'This is Charlie West.'

A woman on the other line, said, 'Hold for President Spender.'

I snorted. I wasn't sure what the joke was, but it was some kind of joke for certain. President Spender – as in the President of the United States of America – wasn't calling me. Obviously.

Only he was.

'This is President Spender,' said the next voice on the phone – and it was really him, too; I recognized his voice.

My back got very straight, so straight it ached. And I said something like, 'Uh . . . Hi . . . Hello . . . Sir . . . Mr President.'

To be honest, I don't really remember exactly what the President said after that. I was kind of in a daze the whole time he was talking. He said he was proud of me, I remember, grateful for what I'd done. He said the American people would be grateful, too, when they found out what had happened.

And, oh yeah, I do remember one point pretty clearly. At one point, President Spender said, 'I want you to know that, when you're ready, there's going to be a place waiting for you in the Air Force Academy. I have some pull with them, being

Commander-in-Chief and all. But listen, I can only get you in the door. After that, you're going to have to make the grade yourself.'

After the President said goodbye, I set the phone down and just sort of stood there. I stared at the phone and thought to myself, *That was the President. Of the United States. Calling me.* Which – come on – was cool.

The door opened. Rose came back in, clumsily manuevering his cast and crutch into the room.

'That was the President,' I told him. 'Of the United States. Calling me.'

Rose nodded. 'Cool.'

'He says he'll get me into the Air Force Academy.'

'Well, he *is* Commander-in-Chief,' said Rose. 'That'll probably count for something.'

I blinked, still trying to take it all in. 'Does this mean I don't have to go back to prison?' I asked him.

I think that was the first time I ever saw Rose just crack up, just lose it. He let out a wild, high laugh, looking down at the floor, shaking his head, his shoulders going up and down with his laughter.

'What?' I said. 'What's so funny? What about all the negotiations and the secrecy and the people who don't want to believe the Homelanders exist?'

It took him another second or so to get back into Serious-Rose mode. When he did, he limped across the room to me. He reached out and put his free hand on my shoulder. He looked at me with his smart, serious eyes.

ANDREW KLAVAN

'You don't have to worry about that anymore, Charlie,' he said. 'Those people's opinions are what you might call "out of fashion" at the moment.'

When I still didn't totally understand, Rose patted my shoulder and said, 'It's over, Charlie. You did it. You stopped them. It's done.'

Now Rose and I walked together to the elevators. There were other people waiting to ride, but a patrolman asked them to take the next car so we could ride down alone. Rose and I stood together as the elevator sank slowly to the ground floor. I didn't say anything at first. I was just trying to get my head around it all.

It was over, like Rose said. No more Homelanders trying to kill me. No more police trying to arrest me. No more days and nights on the run, alone, afraid, confused about who I was and what was happening.

'Where are we going now?' I asked Rose.

He glanced over at me. For a second, I thought he might start laughing again. But no chance. 'Home, Charlie,' he said. 'You, anyway – you're going home.'

Before I could fully comprehend what Rose had said, the elevator touched down. The doors drew open. And suddenly, lights began flashing in my eyes and people started shouting at me. There was a crowd of reporters, waiting in the hospital lobby, taking pictures and video, calling out questions. A confusing chaos of light and noise.

'Can you tell us what happened, Charlie?'

278

'What was it like infiltrating the Homelanders?'

'What happened in the subways last night?'

A couple of patrolmen guided the shouting reporters out of my way. Rose took me by the arm with his free hand. The reporters went on shouting at me as I pushed past them.

They would go on shouting at me for days, in fact. But the stories that were on the news were never the real story – never the whole story. Still, they were enough to clear my name so people understood I hadn't killed my friend or betrayed my country or any of the other stuff I was accused of. That was enough for me. That was more than enough.

When I got past the reporters, I saw the front doors of the hospital. They were all made of glass and the sun was shining through them. It was like walking into a pool of light. I started toward it. But, before I got there, I saw a long black car pull up in the circular driveway outside. Even before the car came to a full stop, its doors started opening. I stood still and stared as my mom and dad and Beth and my sister Amy and my friends Josh and Rick and Miler all poured out of the car and started hurrying to the hospital entrance.

As I went on standing there, amazed, the reporters pushed back toward me. The police made them keep their distance but they formed a half circle around me. Their cameras flashed again, and their bright lights shone on me, and their shouted questions became one loud rush of voices.

At the same time, my family and my friends came through the front doors and hurried to me. Beth reached me first and I threw my arms around her and held her close and then the others were all around me and then . . .

But you know, really, there's nothing else I can say. There are things you can describe in life and things you just can't. There are dangers and adventures, miseries and fears that you can tell about and then . . . well, then there's home and joy and love – and those are beyond the power of words to describe.

So I guess this story is over.